ANNIE M P SMITHSON (1873-1948) was the most successful of all Irish romantic novelists. Her nineteen books, including *The Walk of a Queen, Her Irish Heritage, The Marriage of Nurse Harding* and *The Weldons of Tibradden* were all bestsellers, with their wholesome mix of old-fashioned romance, spirited characters and commonsense philosophy.

She was born in Sandymount, Co Dublin, and reared in the strict Unionist tradition. On completion of her training as a nurse in London and Edinburgh, she returned to Dublin and was posted north as a Queen's Nurse in 1901. Here, for the first time, she experienced the divide between Irish Nationalists and Unionists, and it appalled her. She converted to Catholicism at the age of 34 and was subsequently disowned by most of her family. She immersed herself in the Republican movement — actively canvassing for Sinn Féin in the 1918 General Election, nursing Dubliners during the influenza epidemic of that year, instructing Cumann na mBan on nursing care and tending the wounded of the Civil War in 1922. She was arrested and imprisoned, and threatened to go on hunger-strike unless released.

Forced to resign her commission in the strongly Loyalist Queen's Nurses Committee, she took up private work and tended the poor of Dublin city until she retired in 1942. During her long career, she did much to improve the lot of the nursing profession and championed its cause as Secretary of the Irish Nurses Union.

In later years, she devoted herself to her writing and was an active member of WAAMA, PEN and the Old Dublin Society. Her autobiography, *Myself — and Others*, was completed in 1944, four years before her death at the age of 75.

The Marriage of Nurse Harding

By
ANNIE M. P. SMITHSON

THE MERCIER PRESS
CORK

The Mercier Press, Cork

First published by The Talbot Press

This edition 1989
© The Mercier Press, 1989

British Library Cataloguing in Publication Data
Smithson, Annie M.P., *1873 - 1948*
    The marriage of Nurse Harding.
    I. Title
    823'.912 [F]

    ISBN 978-1-78117-926-0

Typeset by: Seton Music Graphics Ltd., Bantry, Co. Cork.

Transferred to Digital Print-on-Demand in 2024

CONTENTS

CHAPTER 1

HOW IT ALL BEGAN

It all began many years ago, when the present century was in its early infancy. A different place was the world in those days before the Great War had changed the map of Europe, causing thrones to crash, and the blood of millions to be spilt like water; it was a world where motor cars were comparatively few in number; where the cry of 'Votes for Women!' was listened to with amusement or contempt; where careers for girls were limited, and Mrs Grundy was still a personage to be placated.

On a certain morning in those old days—the 1st of June 1901, to be exact—Anne Hewdon looked out of her bedroom window and saw Patrick Dempsey, 'the gardener's boy', going by in the direction of the kitchen garden.

It was just eight o'clock and Anne was standing before her mirror, brushing her hair, which fell in heavy masses over her shoulders. As Pat Dempsey went by, she suspended operations, and, brush in hand, stood gazing after him, while he, totally unaware of her glance, walked leisurely on his way.

He was about twenty, tall, but carried himself badly, slouching along, swinging his arms. 'That fellow needs drilling!' remarked the Colonel one day. Patrick was fair complexioned with auburn hair, and good teeth; the lips were full, the mouth weak. Still he had a debonair manner, and a 'way with him', so that all the girls around were after him. He was a stranger in the district having come from the County Galway.

Anne Hewdon gazed after his retreating figure in silence, a queer expression on her face, until he turned the corner out of sight. Then she hastily finished dressing and went down to breakfast.

Her father, Colonel George Hewdon, was standing by the open window, speaking to Michael Brennan, the gardener. The Colonel was devoted to his garden, and the grounds and gardens attached to Ballafagh House were the pride and joy of his heart.

His wife was already seated at the breakfast table behind the big silver teapot. Louisa Hewdon was a tall, stately woman of fifty, cold, proud, unbending. Neither of her two children could ever remember any caress from her, other than a formal kiss night and morning. They would never have dreamt of running to her in any of their childish troubles; by no stretch of the imagination could one picture Louisa Hewdon running to 'kiss the place and make it well.' All that kind of thing was left to Molly, their nurse, and she naturally went to the other extreme, adoring both children, and doing her best to spoil them.

'Come, George—the bacon will be cold!'

Obediently the Colonel turned from the window and took his place at the table. He had been a brave soldier with a fine record in the Army; in his regiment, although the men liked him, they looked upon him as rather a martinet. But in his own home it was his wife who gave the orders, and the Colonel who obeyed.

He pinched Anne's ear as he passed her chair. He was very fond of his daughter, and found it hard to believe that she was now a young lady of twenty-four. How quickly the years did fly to be sure!

His wife did not forget Anne's age, nor let the girl forget it. This morning she gave her a peculiar look, as she remarked:

'Have you heard that Captain Ogilvy is engaged to Eileen Knox?'

'Yes, mother—I know.'

'What's that?' asked the Colonel.

'I was saying to Anne that Captain Ogilvy, who has been staying with the Crawfords, is engaged to be married to Eileen Knox.'

'Indeed? Oh, well, I hope he does not regret it. That young lady is said to be a bit of a tartar!'

'Still she has secured a husband and a good home. I hear he is well off. Some girls seem to be always left behind.'

At the acid tones Anne flushed vividly. She knew that her mother was bitterly disappointed that she had not married before this. Somehow no one had ever asked her. No one. The girl herself sometimes wondered why this was so? Certainly she was not a beauty, but neither was she very plain. Just an ordinary, healthy girl, rather tall, loose limbed, inclined to be angular; light brown eyes, light brown hair—if they had both been a shade darker, how much prettier she would have looked! Her teeth were perfect, her mouth a bit on the large size. Her figure, with that tendency to angularity, was the worst feature about her, for in those days a plump girl, possessing soft curves, was admired, while the thin ones were laughed at. Anne knew that as she grew older she would become more angular; thinner too—like Aunt Evelina.

She turned her glance in the direction of Miss Evelina Hewdon, the Colonel's sister. This lady was about sixty, some years older than her brother. She was certainly angular, and also certainly plain, both in features and attire. When her elder brother, James Hewdon, had been alive she had lived with him as mistress of Ballafagh House, for James was unmarried. When he died at a comparatively early age, the younger brother, George, who was in India with his regiment, succeeded to the property, and Evelina, who had only a couple of hundred a year of her own, continued to stay on at Ballafagh House. With the difference that she was no longer the mistress.

Yet strange to say, and decidedly to the Colonel's surprise, Miss Hewdon and his wife got on remarkably well together. Perhaps Miss Evelina knew on which side her bread was buttered, and did not fancy exchanging the ease and plenty of Ballafagh House—to which she had been used all her life—for the inconvenience of a boarding house or private hotel. At all events, the present mistress and the former one, were very good friends, and never had the slightest disagreement.

But Anne, looking upon the plain face and generally unattractive appearance of her aunt, found herself thinking that perhaps some day, she too, might be an elderly spinster—horrid appellation!—depending upon her brother, and obliged to be carefully polite to his wife. Victor Hewdon, who was a few years younger than Anne, was in Dublin, reading for the Bar. It was his own wish and a big disappointment to his father who wished him to go into the Army. Victor, however, thought otherwise, and got his own way in the end. When the Colonel died, Victor would succeed to the property which was strictly entailed. Anne would have nothing but whatever provision her father could make for her, and that would not be large, for the income from the estate was comparatively small, and the expense of keeping it in good repair, and the gardens and grounds as he liked to have them was heavy. He knew he could depend upon Victor to see that Louisa was well cared for, because the boy adored his handsome mother, and although she never showed her feelings, it is probable that if she did care for anyone, Louisa Hewdon loved her son.

But Anne was different. The Colonel felt that he would like to leave her enough to live upon in a quiet way, so that she could be independent of her relations. He would prefer to see her happily married, but did not share his wife's anger because the girl had not 'gone off' before this. In fact he would have been very sorry to lose her, and privately thought that it would be hard to find a man good enough for his 'little girl'.

'I am driving into Larramore before lunch—will you come, Anne?' he asked now. She assented gladly, she always enjoyed a drive with her father.

'Right! I'll be leaving in about an hour.'

After breakfast, Anne went into the kitchen garden. There, at the end, where the big pear tree grew against the south wall, she had a plot of her own, where she grew what she liked. She had her father's love of gardening. Here she planted and sowed and watered, getting little help from Michael who considered it so much ground wasted. This morning she stood to admire her roses just coming into bloom, and then noticed how many weeds had sprung up after the rain of the past few days.

Presently Pat Dempsey came by and she called to him.

'Pat! Come here! I want you to help me with the weeds—just look at them!'

As he came over, she wondered what queer impulse had made her call him.

'They're terrible, sure enough! Miss,' he replied, as he stooped down to help her. He was not at all shy, she thought, not like the other garden boys, who had always seemed quite frightened when she spoke to them.

'How long are you here now?' she asked.

'Two months, Miss.'

'Do you like it?'

'Aye—I like it all right.'

'Would you not like to go to America?'

'Well, I might, Miss—and then again, I might not.'

The girl laughed.

'That is a safe way of replying,' she said; 'but you would make money out there, you know.'

'Yes, Miss, so they do be sayin'. But there's no wan but meself, it's not as if I had a father or mother lookin' to me. I have no wan.'

'Are your parents dead, then?'

'Yes, Miss. The two of them died when I was a week or two old. I never heard just what it was—a fever or something that was goin' at the time. I have no relations at all.'

How queer, thought Anne. Most of the people round here have so many relations that they can hardly count them!

'Who brought you up, then?' she asked, 'and looked after you when you were a baby?'

The young fellow was silent for a moment. An expression, as of the memory of some past fear, crossed his face.

'I was sent to Mrs Doherty, Miss,' he said.

'And who might Mrs Doherty be?' she asked, with a laugh.

'She was an awful woman, Miss. She took childer like meself. She had three more besides me, and we used to be beat and murdered black and blue—half starved too we were. I was there till I was seven years old, and then—something happened.'

'Yes—what was it?'

'There was meself and young Dicky Doyle. The other child had died. Then another came—a baby a few weeks old, and it fell out of her arms into the fire wan day when she had drink taken, and it was burnt alive.'

'Oh!' breathed Anne, feeling quite sick for the moment.

'Yes, Miss. And it was me tried to save the poor infant—she was too drunk herself to do anything. It was lying right on top of the fire——'

'Please—don't tell me any more!'

'No, Miss. Well, a lady—some kind of inspector, came round, the police wid her, and ould Doherty got jail, and me and Dicky Doyle were sent to an industrial school. It was there I learnt about gardening and so on, and when I was sixteen I was sent to Sir George Dare's place—near Galway town. It was there I got to know Jim McGrath, and when the family went to foreign parts, he got me this situation with Mr Brennan.'

'You should write a history of your life, Pat, it is like a story.'

'Oh, sure it's jokin' you are, Miss.'

'No, indeed, I am not. And now tell me, which of the places do you like the best? The school or Sir George Dare's or here?'

'I like this, Miss.'

'Oh, I'm so glad you do! And I hope that Michael is decent to you?'

'Is it Mr Brennan, Miss?'

'Yes,' laughingly; 'and here he is! Michael!'

'Miss?'

Brennan came towards them, a tall, lean man, tanned by the sun and rain, devoted to his garden, a 'divil for work' according to the various boys who had worked under him.

'I have been talking to Pat,' said Anne.

'Yes, Miss?' casting a look at Pat as if he would ask if he had nothing better to do than idle his time 'weeding' Miss Anne's rubbishy patch.

'You need not think he is wasting time,' quick to notice Michael's expression. 'I called him to help me, and he has been telling me about his life. He has had a hard time, Michael, and I do hope you are kind to him?'

The gardener's face was a study in expression. He looked at Anne as if he half suspected that she was making fun of him, but as she seemed perfectly serious, he turned his gaze upon Pat, and that young man guessed pretty accurately that Miss Anne's intercession would have the opposite effect to what she hoped.

'Very good, Miss,' replied Michael, in a non-committal manner; 'when you have finished with him, will you send him to me in the green-house?' and with another glance at the unhappy Pat, the gardener shouldered his spade and went off.

'Is he cross with you, Pat?'

The voice was kind, and the boy meeting her eyes was astonished to see how soft they were.

'Oh, no, Miss—only an odd time! But if you wouldn't mind I think I'd better go after him now.'

'You will go when I have finished with you—not before! I want you to tell me some more about Mrs Doherty.'

'I could not indeed, Miss—it wouldn't be fit talk for a lady like yourself.'

Anne was about to insist, but to Pat's relief, the Colonel's voice was suddenly heard calling for Anne.

'Goodness! I forgot I was to go into Larramore with Daddy—I must fly!'

'A lovely young lady, right enough!' thought Pat Dempsey, looking after her; 'faith—if she was a girl of me own kind I wouldn't be long about giving her a good hug—I would not! Quare and nice she was to talk to, too, but I'd just as lief she hadn't said anything to Mr Brennan—and that's the truth!'

'And let ye attend to yer own business for the future, and not be so eager to go runnin' after Miss Anne. Weedin' and the like! Child's play—that's what it is, and plenty of rale weedin' waitin' to be done. D'ye hear me now?'

'I do, Mr Brennan.'

'Well, let ye take heed to what I say!'

Meanwhile Anne had joined her father, and was presently sitting beside him in the dog cart, bowling along the road to Larramore with Mab, the grey mare between the shafts, and the hedges fragrant with wild roses and honeysuckle, rushing past them. The town of Larramore was about three miles from Ballafagh House. The road was good, the June day warm and pleasant, and as a rule Anne would be chatting away as they spun along.

But today she was very quiet, so silent, indeed, that her father asked: 'Is anything the matter, Anne? You do not seem like yourself. Got a headache?'

'Oh, I'm all right, Daddy—don't worry!'

Silence again, broken by the Colonel saying, jocosely, 'So Miss Eileen Knox has got a husband at last?'

He had spoken for the mere sake of conversation, and was astonished when his daughter turned upon him angrily.

'Oh, for Goodness sake—didn't Mother say enough about that without you starting it!'

'My dear——'

Amazement almost bereft him of speech.

'Well—I mean it! How can I help it if men don't ask me to marry them? I am on view often enough! Mother drags me everywhere that a man is likely to be found. Oh, I am so sick of it all!'

She was furious and did not want to cry, but, in spite of herself, angry tears choked her utterance. Her father, amazed, vexed beyond words, drew the dog cart to the side of the road and put his arms around her.

'Now what in the world is all this about? Surely you don't think for one moment that we want to lose you? Why, Anne, I have often dreaded the day when you would marry and leave us—perhaps to go far away. What would I do without my little girl?'

'Mother would be glad. She is always throwing it in my face that I am not married before this. You know Daddy, I am twenty-four.

You heard what she said at breakfast about Captain Ogilvy and Eileen Knox. Oh, why can't girls earn their own living and be independent like boys? Look at Victor—what a good time he has!'

'But my dear girl, surely you don't want to go away to Dublin and live by yourself?'

'I wouldn't mind if I could earn enough to keep me.'

'Good Lord, child—you are not going to be a Suffragette, are you?'

'I would like to be independent. It is horrid to think that marriage is the only way by which a woman can attain a position and have a home of her own.'

'Well, certainly, my dear, in our class of life, it is usual for girls to marry. I mean it is the happier life. An old maid is seldom wanted by anyone. Look at your aunt for instance. She is all right, of course, in a manner of speaking, but I often think how much nicer a woman she would have been with a home and children. Oh, yes— marriage is best for women.'

'That's all very fine, Daddy, but you know that there are more women than men in the world—in fact there are not enough men to go round! What are the rest of the girls to do—join the Mormons?'

The Colonel laughed, and seeing that Anne was now more herself shook up the reins and the mare started off again along the country road.

'You see, my dear,' he said, presently, 'the girls of the lower classes work—often after their marriage, too. Especially in the factories in England; here, of course, we have not so much of that sort of work—not in County Mayo anyway! And then girls of a better class are going in for a University education —great rubbish in my opinion—trying to be doctors and dentists and so on! But that won't go on—they are sure to be failures. The best job that I know of for women is nursing. But the training in hospital is hard.'

'Could I be a nurse, Daddy?'

'You could not—never with my permission. No, no, Anne, my dear. If you meet a man you like and he likes you—well, marry him by all means. But I will not have you coerced in any way, and as for being independent, I hope to be able to leave you enough to live upon.'

'Oh, Daddy—don't! Please don't! If anything happened to you, I would die too—I would not want to live!'

'Stuff and nonsense, little girl! You are beginning your life, and must not say such things. As for me, I am not very old, and hope to see a few years more. Indeed I want to—particularly for your sake, as I wish to be able to put a little by for you every year.'

'Now, Daddy, say no more! You are to live to be a hundred and ten—and I will wheel you about in a bath chair. I will be a nice old maid! I am going to eat a lot of butter to try and get fat. Don't you think a plump old maid would be nice for a change?'

Her father patted her hand.

'Old or young, plump or thin, to me you will always be my own little girl,' he said.

CHAPTER II

A DRIVE TO LARRAMORE

The town of Larramore lay sleepy and quiet this June day. It was not a busy place at any time, with the one exception of Fair days and Christmas. On Fair days all was bustle and confusion; cattle and pigs straying from the street to the side path; the drivers yelling and shouting; farmers and their wives buying and selling, driving hard bargains both ways; every public house crammed to overflowing; every kind of vehicle, with every kind of animal in the shafts, waiting patiently for the return of their owners—the more prosperous turnouts being put up in the yards of the hotels and public-houses, while the humbler ass and cart stood under archways or beside railings, the patient little donkeys safely tethered with bits of rope or string.

Anne liked those Fair days. At least there was some sign of life in the town then. Today it might have been the town of the Sleeping Beauty—without the Beauty.

Sergeant O'Brien, of the R.I.C., taking his ease outside the barrack, sprang smartly to attention as Colonel Hewdon drove by. Acknowledging his salute, the Colonel turned the mare's head in the direction of the principal street, and a moment later, drew up before the bank.

'You had better wait for me—Mab seems a bit fresh,' and jumping down he threw the reins to his daughter.

'All right, Daddy. But I think Mab is quiet enough—it's only on Fair days that she gets excited.'

'I won't be long anyhow,' and her father disappeared within the portals of the bank.

Anne, reins loosely held, sat watching the few passers by, receiving and replying to various salutations. There was Pat O'Byrne, the baker, standing at the door of his shop, from whence issued a most appetising smell of fresh bread; opposite, was the butcher—a shop which she detested, so like a shambles did it seem, with its wooden blocks, and bleeding carcasses. The butchers of that time, in such country towns, did not present an attractive display. But

Dan Molloy was a most cheery man himself, smiling, good-natured, so that it seemed almost impossible to imagine him killing a fly—much less a dear little lamb.

'How deceptive appearances can be!' thought Anne. 'Oh, dear, here is Dr McHale.'

The doctor was coming out of his house, just across the street. He was a short, stout man, with a brown beard, of average capabilities, he was hardworking and conscientious. But he had—in common with his wife—one failing. He was a bit of a snob and liked nothing so much as to be seen talking to any of the 'country' people, or visiting at their houses. As the Hewdons undoubtedly belonged to that category, he now hastened across to the dog cart, hand outstretched.

'My dear Miss Hewdon—this is a pleasure! I suppose the Colonel is in the bank? Would you not come in and rest? Mrs McHale would be so glad.'

'Thank you, Doctor, but Daddy will be out in a minute, and I don't like to leave the mare—she is not to be trusted.'

'I will send my boy——'

'Oh, no—it is not worth while. How is Mrs McHale?'

'She is well, and will be sorry to have missed you—why I declare, here she is herself! She must have seen you from the window.'

Which is precisely what his better half had done.

Mary McHale was a thin little woman of middle-age, grey haired, with traces of a youthful prettiness still remaining. She was the mother of twelve children, ten of whom were alive, and only she, herself, knew the struggle it had been to feed, clothe and educate such a family on the salary of a dispensary doctor. Needless to add, every paying case was a godsend, and great was the rivalry between Dr McHale and the other medical man, Dr Doyle. Of the two, Dr McHale had the bigger practice—and he certainly wanted it.

His wife came forward now, all smiles.

'Dear Miss Hewdon—do come in and have a glass of wine—or would you prefer a cup of tea? The girls would be so charmed to have a little chat.'

'Thank you so much, Mrs McHale—but here comes my father.' For, much to her relief, Anne had caught sight of the Colonel leaving the bank, accompanied to the door by Peter Richards, the manager. On seeing Anne, he too, came over to the dog cart, and much laughter and light badinage followed.

'And so Miss Knox is engaged to Captain Ogilvy,' remarked Mrs McHale, 'I hear he is extremely wealthy. She is a very lucky girl!'

'Well, that is as it may be,' said Colonel Hewdon, with a quick glance at his daughter, 'she really knows but little of the man. He has been a visitor here for a couple of months, and has to rejoin his regiment in India almost immediately.'

'Oh—but I am sure she will be happy! To be rich—able to travel——' Words failed her, and Mary McHale sighed instead, thinking of her seven daughters, whose ages ranged from ten to twenty-six—and not one of them off her hands yet! If Delia or Mollie, the two eldest, did not marry soon, they would have to think of something they could do to help the family exchequer. It has hard they had had no offers, and they had been to Dublin too, for several visits. Her married sister there had done her best for them, but with no result. Yes—a lucky girl was Eileen Knox. But, of course, she was 'county', and had more opportunities of meeting people— the best kind too. Ah, well! Perhaps their luck might turn yet—she could only hope for the best.

Anne, too, thought that Eileen was a lucky girl. Money—travel— change of scene.

'Day dreaming, Miss Hewdon?' asked the bank manager, jocularly, 'you will be the next young lady to go off across the seas with a rich husband—and leave all the other girls dying of envy!'

Suddenly catching sight of the doctor's wife regarding him with none too pleasant a glance, Richards realised he had 'put his foot in it', and muttering that a man was waiting for him, shook hands with Anne hastily, and retreated into the safe shelter of the bank.

'Where to, now?' asked the Colonel, goodbyes being at last said to the McHales.

'Mother has given me a list of things she wants at McCarthy's.'

That done, they went to the shop that supplied them with periodicals and magazines, and having laid in a good supply, turned the mare's head towards home once more.

'I will be glad of my lunch,' remarked the Colonel, 'I feel more than a bit peckish.'

'Well—you could have had a glass of wine from Mrs McHale.'

'Thanks—no! I have tasted the stuff before. Not that she does not mean well. She is a nice little thing and must have had the deuce of a struggle to rear the family on the doctor's income.'

Anne, with the intolerance of youth, was not much interested in the McHales and their money troubles. For a moment her father was silent, but then he went on:

'Yes—she deserves great credit. You know, Anne, financial worry is the devil! Especially when one has appearances to keep up. When I was in India, and your mother and I were first married, I had only a hundred a year, besides my pay. When you two children came along, it was just all I could do to make ends meet. I got promotion and better pay, but we had to keep up a good style, and your mother, as wife of the head of the regiment, had to dress well. And I was always trying to save a little because I believed that poor George would marry some day. I often said to your mother that he would bring home a girl in her teens to be mistress of Ballafagh House, and perhaps if he had lived he might have done so. However, he didn't. He died—fairly young, too—and here am I now in his place. Poor George—I never envied him his birthright— and was sorry enough when I heard of his death.'

'Oh, Daddy! Look what is coming! A circus!'

A circus it was, one of those third-rate shows which travel the country parts of Ireland, with a few caravans, worn out horses, a mangy bear, a monkey or two. This particular one was to open in the town of Larramore that evening, and was now making its way slowly along the road, two white horses with long tails drawing the caravans—the same horses that later on would curvet gently round the arena, while Mademoiselle de Villette—in ordinary life Mrs Nan McGarry—rode through hoops and performed other feats of equestrian skill. Quiet, inoffensive animals they were, but Mab, the mare, seemed to resent their advent. She twitched her ears, showed the whites of her eyes, and began to prance and rear, like the nervous lady that she was.

'Easy, easy, old girl—what's the matter?' soothed the Colonel.

Mab was quieting down a little and all might have been well had the dog cart been allowed to proceed on its way without interference. Unfortunately, one of the clowns, seeing these two, so evidently belonging to the 'quality' and scenting future patrons—the best seats, too—ran forward, waving a flag, and at the same time, letting off a series of 'slap bangs', right in front of the mare. Accustomed to horses who would not turn a hair if a gun went off beside them, the man had no idea of the effect that his silly act would have on the well-bred nervous animal coming towards him.

The mare, aghast, terrified out of her wits, reared on to her hind legs, and then bolted, scattering the circus folk in all directions, while she tore straight in front of her, speeding down the road, like an arrow from its bow, unheeding, unseeing, blind from terror, with but one objective to fly from the awful thing which had sprung from nowhere with such frightful suddenness.

Anne, sitting upright, clinging to her seat, teeth clenched, wondered how long this mad gallop would last? Wondered, too, what would eventually stop Mab in her mad flight? Surely she must tire soon! The Colonel was standing, pulling on the reins with all his strength, but it seemed to make no difference. The animal sped ahead, her speed undiminished.

Fortunately the road was clear in front of them, not a thing in sight.

'Heaven grant it stays so!' breathed Anne.

Her prayer was not to be granted. Presently they turned a corner—Anne had known that corner was coming, dreaded it, wondering what it might bring—and there, right in the middle of the road stood a cart full of stones. The tail end of the cart faced them, and the horse harnessed to it was so old, so worn out, that even the rattle of the dog-cart tearing down the road behind him, did not cause him to turn his head.

Two men were sitting by the roadside, enjoying a pipe. The noise of the rushing vehicle, the stones flying beneath the mare's feet, roused them to a realisation of the run-away. But before they could make any effort to stop her, had this been possible, the crash had come. The mare, with a scream like a soul in torment, reared upright, and then fell to the ground, dragging the dog-cart with her.

To Anne, there came a merciful oblivion.

●   ●   ●

'Well—it's no use talking—but I cannot tell you how sorry I am! If anything at all could have been done for him—but it was all over when I got there. Of one thing you may rest assured, dear Mrs Hewdon, and that is that he did not suffer.'

'Thank you, Doctor—you are very kind. I am sure you did all you could. I am most grateful.'

'And now a little sleeping draught—just a harmless mixture to quiet the nerves——'

'No, thank you. I am never troubled with nerves.'

'But just to give you a few hours sleep? No? Well, are you sure now there is nothing I can do for you?'

'Nothing more—thank you again. You have been most kind. You think that Anne will be all right?'

'Oh, yes! Nurse Harding is splendid, you may leave her with perfect confidence in her hands. She is already sleeping, and will probably have a good night. It is wonderful that Miss Hewdon escaped with only a broken arm—a simple fracture, too! By the way, you have sent for Mr Hewdon?'

'Yes, I wired at once. He will be here between one and two in the morning—it is nearly one o'clock when his train gets into Larramore. I have arranged for a car to meet him.'

She spoke quietly, but Dr McHale noticed that the mention of sending a car to meet him, had moved her more than she wished him to see. Poor Mab! Never again would she take the dog-cart to meet Victor at the train. A shot from the sergeant's gun had ended her misery.

'Then if I can do no more, I will leave you for the present. My wife was most anxious that I should tell you that if there was anything at all she or the girls could do to help——'

'That is very kind—please thank her—but for the moment there is nothing.'

To herself, Louisa Hewdon was saying: 'If he would go—if he would only go!' And go he did at last, good, well-meaning man, used to the noisy demonstrations of grief from most of his patients, and baffled, puzzled by this woman, so quiet, so self-controlled.

Always a reserved woman, one who never allowed her feelings to be seen, the shock of the past few hours had left little mark upon Mrs Hewdon, except that her face was paler than usual. It is probable that she hardly realised as yet the fact that her husband was dead—killed, as it were, in a moment of time. She was not conscious of any grief, any sorrow. She was simply numb, incapable of any feeling, save the physical one of intense cold.

Eight o'clock. Five hours since George had been brought home to her. Would she ever be able to forget the sight of the country cart, coming slowly up the avenue of Ballafagh House? She had been standing on the steps, Dr McHale at her side, and she had experienced that queer feeling that most people have at such moments—the feeling that she was watching some scene from a book or play—some incident in the life of a stranger. It did not seem to have anything to do with her at all.

In the bottom of the cart, covered by a rug, lay the body of her husband. Sitting with her back to him, propped up against a rough seat, was Anne, dazed, stupid, in pain from her broken arm, not yet understanding that her father was dead.

Yes, Dr McHale had been kind. She would always remember his kindness. She had never thought much of him, and rather disliked his wife. Not that she had bothered much about her one way or the other. Louisa Hewdon was one of the D'Arcy Brownes, and thought a great deal of her family, being intensely proud and a Conservative of the old school. Her people had considered that she might have made a better match than George Hewdon, then only a younger son with no expectations of succeeding to the Ballafagh property. But Louisa had loved him in her cold, proud way, and she had never had cause to regret her marriage. He had been a good husband in every sense of the word. She would miss him—would feel his loss tremendously when she was capable of realising it. She began to understand this in a dim sort of way already.

'Canon Bowden, madam.'

The parlourmaid, ushering in the clergyman, brought her back to her surroundings. If it had been possible she would not have seen him, but no doubt the maid had thought she would like to see the Rector.

'My dear Mrs Hewdon—I am distressed, grieved beyond words! Sit down, I beg of you. The shock must have been terrible—"In the midst of life"—how true it is!'

She replied politely, knowing that she must listen to what he would be sure to say on such an occasion, agree with the usual platitudes, yet knowing too, that at the moment they meant nothing to her.

Canon Bowden, although he had expected that she would take her loss quietly, was astonished at her self-control. Only by her pallor, her careful repression of anything approaching emotion, did he guess that she was suffering.

'And Anne? How is she? A broken arm, I hear?'

'Yes. Nurse Harding is with her, and Anne is sleeping—Dr McHale gave her a draught. He set her arm and says she will be all right.'

'You have sent for Victor?'

'Yes, he will be here by the late train—about half-past one in the morning.'

A few more stereotyped phrases, messages of sympathy from his wife, a promise to call in the morning to see Victor—'there will be the funeral arrangements of course, but no need to trouble her with them'—and then he too, went away and she was alone once more.

If it had been Anne who had been killed instead of George? She almost found herself wishing that this had been so. She knew that she ought not to wish it, her daughter was young, her life before her. Yet, somehow or other, mother and daughter had never been in harmony with each other, and later on, their wills would be sure to clash. If only Anne were married! How different Victor was! Never could she imagine herself wishing that he would go away— or even marry. She wished he could have been with her today. He would have been a rock of strength.

Here was Hayes again, eyes reddened, face swollen. The Colonel had been a good master.

'No—I do not want any dinner, thank you, Hayes, but you might ask cook to send me up some soup—only a little. And see that Nurse Harding has all she requires for the night. Of course, cook knows that'—she was going to say 'Master Victor', for so he was usually called by the household, but suddenly changed the words—'Mr Hewdon will be here about half-past one?'

'Yes, madam—we all know.'

'Then you will see that everything is ready for him...'

That was all, and Hayes went downstairs to marvel in company with the other servants, at the wonderful way in which the mistress was 'bearing up'.

'But sure herself was always a hard wan,' said Mary Ellen, the kitchen maid.

'Let ye hould yer tongue about the mistress,' reprimanded the cook, 'and remember that it's them that says the least that feels the most.'

The old house was quiet, with the quietness that King Death always brings with him when he enters. Downstairs, the servants talked in whispers round the kitchen fire; in the breakfast room, where she was waiting for Victor, and where she had had the table set and a fire lit, Louisa Hewdon sat motionless, hour by hour; in the room just overhead, Anne lay sleeping, Nurse Harding watching her and thinking her own thoughts; while in the big bedroom across the corridor, was all that remained of George Hewdon.

Suddenly Nurse Harding lifted her head, and going to the window gazed out into the moonlit night. To her ears had come the sound of a horse and car driving rapidly up the avenue, the next moment it had come in sight—was at the door. No need to knock or ring, the door was flung open and footsteps crossed the wide hall—footsteps which were familiar to Nurse Harding. The window of the breakfast room must have been open, too, for a cry was carried to her ears from the room beneath.

'Victor—my son—'

'Mother—darling mother—'

Very softly, Nurse Harding closed the bedroom window, and went back to her seat by her patient.

CHAPTER III

NORA HARDING

Nora Harding, seated in a low chair, book in hand, found herself listening—listening for the sound of Mrs Hewdon's steps coming upstairs to bed. Surely she would look in to see how her daughter was keeping? Would Victor come with her?

Nora Harding was twenty-five, but looked less, even in the fashions of those days which added to a woman's age, instead of taking from it, as do our modern ones. She was of medium height, inclined to be plump, with soft brown hair, growing low on her forehead and piled on top of her head in glossy plaits; her feet and hands were small; the mouth wide, sensitive.

She had come to Larramore a year ago, sent down from the head office in Dublin to take up the post of District Nurse under the local committee of which Lady Larramore—the great lady of the neighbourhood—was the President, and Mrs Hewdon the Hon. Treasurer. Although Nurse Harding's services were primarily intended for the poor of the district, it was an understood thing, that the shop people and others who could afford to pay a subscription to the funds of the Association, would be entitled to make use of her services. And in the case of an emergency like the present, she would be sent for at once, until a nurse was sent down from Dublin, if this were considered necessary.

It was nearly three o'clock, that hour of early dawn, when even in June, the air strikes cold and wan, when Mrs Hewdon at last came up the stairs and down the corridor to her daughter's room. She glanced towards the bed, and seeing that Anne was still sleeping, just asked the nurse if she had everything that she required, and then, with a cold 'goodnight', went to her own room.

Half an hour—three-quarters—went by, and then came the sound for which Nora was listening—waiting. A soft tap at the door. Noiselessly she opened it, and Victor Hewdon entered.

He was a tall young fellow of two and twenty, but so serious and grave for his age that he seemed older than he was. Seeing him with Nora one would have taken him for the elder of the two. He had thick auburn hair, with a natural wave—which same wave was a cause of much heartburning to his sister, as was also the fact that his eyes were just that dark shade of blue which would have so improved her own appearance. He was like Anne, only a handsomer edition.

His glance went first to the bed where she lay, and then to Nurse Harding.

'She's asleep?'

'Yes—the doctor gave her a draught.'

He came nearer to Nora, asking in a whisper: 'Are you sure she is really asleep?'

'Oh, yes—she is still under the effects of the sleeping draught. She will not wake for some hours yet, unless she gets a lot of pain which is not likely.'

'We can talk then. But first, Nora dear—give me a kiss.'

He put his arms around her and kissed her again and again, then, rather wearily, as one who is desperately tired, he sank into a seat opposite to her.

'Do you know, Nora, the thought that you might be here was the one comfort I had when I got the news. It was such a shock. Poor old Dad! Tell me all you know—I did not like to ask mother much about it.'

She told him what she knew about the accident, and could not help noticing that although he felt his father's death acutely, and was sorry for Anne—even sorry too, in a different way for the poor mare who was the cause of the whole thing—yet his chief worry, his whole sympathy, seemed to be for his mother.

'Poor mother!' he said, 'how she will feel it. And I can do so little to help her.'

'You are very fond of your mother?'

'Why, yes, you know that, Nora. I have always loved her—much better than poor old Dad.'

'But she is so cold—so reserved.'

'I know. Still from a small boy I have loved her—kind of worshipped from afar!'

Nora was silent for a space, then she said:

'All this will make a difference to you, Victor?'

'It will. I will be in his place now—I would to God he had lived longer! Why he was only midde-aged, and so strong and active. I feel unequal to taking it all on my shoulders—there's a lot of worry over the estate. But, of course, my mother will help me—she understands all the working of the place.'

Nora made no reply, and he glanced at her quickly. Then leaning forward he put his hand over hers, saying, softly: 'You are thinking this will make a difference to us too—to you and me? But that is nonsense—it will make no difference in the world—how can it? Don't you know that I will never love anyone but you—surely you know that—Nora, my darling?'

'Perhaps. But there is your mother.'

He said nothing, and she went on: 'You know that Mrs Hewdon would never even contemplate the idea for a moment—she would not dream of allowing us to marry. I am a district nurse, no money, and although,' with a twinkle in her eye—'I may be fairly respectable, I certainly am not "county!" She is, and does not forget it—and will not let you forget it either. No, we may as well give it all up, Victor—we will never be allowed to marry.'

'I will never give you up. I know that my mother will not be pleased, and at first she may cut up a bit rusty. But afterwards she will come round all right. Just you wait and see!'

'I do not believe it—it is useless to think of it! I know it, Victor. Something tells me that we will have to part.'

'I will never give you up, of that you may rest assured,' he replied again.

'Well, we will not speak any more about it now,' she said, quietly, 'and it is best for you to go to bed and try to get some sleep.'

'And what about you? You have been up all day—or rather yesterday, as it is now!'

'Oh, I'm used to it! All in the day's work. If I wasn't here, I would probably be somewhere else! Go, now, and lie down.'

He kissed her again, tenderly, gravely, and went.

Left to herself, waiting for morning, with nothing to do but watch the sleeping girl, Nora Harding went over the past year and her friendship with Victor Hewdon.

She remembered how she had first met him. It had been at a Garden Fête, given at Ballafagh House by Mrs Hewdon, in aid of the funds of the Nursing Association. Nora had been asked to attend—quite a polite invitation, but that it was really in the form of a Royal Command, she knew perfectly well. Of course, she was expected to wear uniform, and did so—dark linen frock, white apron, cuffs and collar, neat little bonnet tied with the dinkiest of bows under her pretty chin. Such was the uniform of the District Nurse of 1901... And it suited the feminine charms of Nurse Harding, so that Victor, seeing her for the first time, thought that he had seldom seen such a lovely girl.

He was home for the summer holidays, and his mother had commandeered his help for the Tea Tent. Nora was there, too, going back and forth with trays and teapots, waiting impartially upon both the county and townspeople, all gathered there because Mrs Hewdon of Ballafagh had asked them. Many of them were members of the Nursing Association, and to these she had to be especially nice. The day was hot, she was tired and weary and wished it was over so that she might get home and rest and make a cup of tea for herself—no one had thought of offering her one here.

Then she had seen that good-looking boy, Mrs Hewdon's son, coming towards her. She had noticed him all the afternoon, flying around like herself, with tea and cake, but no one had introduced her to him, and indeed, she had been too busy to think much about him. But now he was smiling, had taken a tray from her, passing it on to a maid from the house, giving her some directions at the same time. Then to Nora: 'You are tired and hot, I have put Mary in charge now—nearly all the teas are finished. It's high time you and your humble assistant—my poor self!—should have some refreshment, too!'

He guided her to a quiet place in the grounds, and there presently Mary brought them tea.

'You are Nurse Harding, of course,' he said; 'perhaps you know my name?'

'Yes—you are Mr Hewdon.'

'Generally known as Victor to my friends—and we must be friends after our strenuous labours together this afternoon!'

And so had started a friendship that was soon to merge into a deeper, warmer feeling. They met often. Nora did most of her rounds on a bicycle, having long distances to go. Victor, too, had a machine, and it was surprising how frequently they met on the lonely country roads, cycling together for miles.

No word of their intimacy reached the ears of Mrs Hewdon, but, in any case, she would never have dreamt for a moment of Victor falling in love with the District Nurse. She, herself, seldom saw Nora, except when she would send for her to Ballafagh House, to ask her for details about some patient in whom she was interested, or when her services were required to attend any of the household for minor ailments. Louisa Hewdon was always polite, even kind, to the District Nurse, but thought of her solely as the paid official of the Nursing Association. She sent Nurse Harding her monthly salary with business-like punctuality, and at stated times told the gardener to send some fruit and vegetables to the nurse's cottage.

Nora received the large salary of £96 per annum, plus free house and coal. It was a pretty cottage, standing by itself at the foot of a hill, just outside the town, and there the nurse lived alone, having a girl in once a week to do the washing and scrubbing. She had to pay Mollie Brady out of her own pocket, so that even in those pre-war days when the cost of living was so much cheaper than it is now, Nora had not found it too easy to make ends meet, and put something by for holidays and the dreaded 'rainy day'.

Still she had managed to pull along and was not unhappy. When she first came to Larramore, she had been very lonely and homesick for Dublin life, but this had worn off by degrees as she grew accustomed to the district, and got to like her patients. Not that they could ever be as dear to her as the Dublin poor, among whom she had worked for a happy six months before being transferred to the west.

And then Victor had come into her life.

She hardly knew when it was that he had first told her that he loved her. Or, indeed, had he ever told her in so many words? Looking back upon those golden summer days which had followed their first meeting, it seemed to her that words were not needed between them; together they dwelt in Arcady, walking hand in hand through that lovely country, while all around shone the 'light that never was on sea or land'.

Every morning her waking thought was: 'Shall I meet him today?' and at night her last thought: 'We will meet tomorrow!' Then he had to return to Dublin, and there followed wretched, lonely days, which held no interest save only the daily call of the postman. She wondered, sometimes, if Paddy Byrne were at all curious about her letters from Dublin? Or the post mistress, Miss Daly? Anyway she did not care. Nothing mattered in the world except just Victor and his love for her.

His letters were charming, a trifle pedantic, perhaps, very sentimental as was the mode at that time; the modern girl would probably laugh at them, but Nora kept them all tied together with ribbon, locked up in her desk, and every night would take out two or three and read them over. When all the letters were finished, she would begin at the beginning and read them through again, and, as their number was rapidly growing, she was never short of reading matter! The heavenly foolishness of youth! The day was to come when Nora could afford a tender little smile for the girl who used to sit up in bed in the nurse's cottage at Larramore, and read and kiss the words which her lover had written.

At Christmas Victor came home again, but although they managed to see one another a few times, they had not the same opportunity as in the summer. Then he had been down again at Easter, for a few days. He had come to see her at the cottage one evening, and they had a serious talk about their future. It was decided that Victor should work hard at his studies and get called to the Bar as soon as possible.

'Then we will marry, Sweetheart—and chance our luck!' She looked at him tenderly but her voice was anxious as she asked: 'Do you think that wise?'

'Why, yes, of course! Once we are married Dàd and Mother will come round all right. They may not like it at first, but I will get on— I am sure of that—and we can live in Dublin until they relent. It will be like a scene from a play or novel!'

They both realised that this marriage would be against the wishes of the Colonel—and particularly against every aim and wish of Mrs Hewdon, who had very different designs for her son. She was a woman, too, of iron will, one whom it would be hard to change. Nora thinking of her, would feel her courage slipping from her. But Victor was always the optimist and kept her heart up, assuring her that all would be well, painting in rosy colours the future which they would have together.

At that time—only two months ago—any thought of the Colonel's death had never crossed their mind. Victor hoped his father would live for many years to come; he wished to continue his studies, to be called to the Bar, to make a career for himself in that profession. Country life did not appeal to him, he preferred living in Dublin, and always thrust on one side the fact—of which his mother often reminded him—that he would one day be master of Ballafagh House, with the duties and responsibilities attached thereto. But his father was barely sixty, still hale and hearty—why should he die? So we all reason, until the King of Terrors, with a grim smile, stalks into our midst, and gathers into his cold arms that one whom we least expected to go—whom we could least afford to lose.

Now all was changed for Victor. The Colonel was dead, and his son must reign in his stead as Master of Ballafagh House and property, must take his place as Hewdon of Ballafagh, next in importance to Lord Larramore himself.

Nora Harding, watching the dawn rise over the hills of Mayo, thought of all these things. That Victor loved her, she knew well, yet even with that knowledge, she had little hope he would be able to marry her. His mother would prevent it. He could not marry in any case for a while, and during that waiting period, Mrs Hewdon would manage in some way to come between them. She would be perfectly furious when she heard about the affair; how Victor would ever find the courage to tell her, Nora could not conceive. Certainly, Victor was resolute, and inherited his mother's strength of will; on the other hand, he was devoted to her, and especially now, he would think it his duty to please her in every possible way. Nora sighed, and the eyes that gazed across the distance to the hills beyond, were rather dim. But suddenly her courage returned to her, and she flung up her head with a resolute air.

'This is nonsense—I am tired out, that is why I feel so wretched. Victor is of age, he is nearly twenty-three—I wish I were not the elder, not that it matters much, I suppose!—and his own master. Surely between us we can settle our own affairs and get married if we like! Anyway, I'm not going to look at the dark side any longer! There's the sun rising over the hills—just as it's going to rise over our lives—Victor's and mine!'

There was a little sound from behind, and Nora, merged at once into the nurse, went swiftly to the bedside, where lay Anne Hewdon, waking at last, dazed and stupid, conscious of physical pain indeed, but as yet ignorant of the tragedy which was to change her whole life.

CHAPTER IV

MOTHER AND SON

They were assembled in the drawingroom, waiting to hear the Will read; Mrs Hewdon, cold, quiet, looking more reserved than ever in her deep mourning; Miss Evelina, eyes and nose swollen and red, sitting upright in a straight backed chair, black-bordered pocket handkerchief in her hand; Anne, lying on a sofa, pale, haggard, and miserable; Victor, seated beside his mother, very grave and serious.

Mr Owen, the solicitor from Larramore, read the Will. It was quite short. The property being strictly entailed, the Colonel had little to leave. There was a legacy of one hundred pounds to 'my dear daughter, Anne.' His wife, he left to the care of his son, Victor, 'as I know he will see that his mother wants for nothing.'

'I must explain a little,' said Mr Owen; 'Colonel Hewdon, against my advice, lately invested a thousand pounds in a certain company which he saw advertised. This investment turned out badly—it was a mere bubble—and the Colonel lost every penny. He felt it very much, as he had hopes of doubling his capital, and so being able to make a better provision for his daughter. As it is now, he had only the hundred pounds to leave her. He had no anxiety about you, Mrs Hewdon, as he knew you would always have a home at Ballafagh, but he was anxious to leave Miss Hewdon some competence in case she did not marry.'

From the sofa, there came a muffled sob, but otherwise complete silence until Mrs Hewdon broke it.

'Am I to understand then, Mr Owen, that my husband has left me nothing—nothing at all?'

'He had nothing to leave, except the small sum which his daughter inherits. You know, Mrs Hewdon, that he has laid out a good deal of money on the estate since he succeeded his brother. There has not been time for the land and gardens to yield the profits he expected, but undoubtedly they will do so in due course. It was a pity about the thousand he lost, but he would not take my advice, and I am afraid he was not a good business man.'

'But to leave me nothing—nothing!'

'Your husband was not anxious about your future, Mrs Hewdon. He knew you would be well cared for, and that in a material sense, his death would make no difference to you.'

And the solicitor turned and bowed to Victor and with old-fashioned courtesy.

The young man went to his mother and kissed her.

'You will not worry over this, mother? You know everything will be all right for you.'

Her eyes searched his face for a moment before she spoke. Then she said: 'Thank God, I have you, Victor—you are all I have now!'

A strange feeling, a sudden dread, came over Victor, keeping him silent. Then he shook himself free from the sensation as he replied: 'Of course you have me, mother—you are not to worry.'

The funeral over, and the blinds drawn up again at Ballafagh House, life resumed its normal course, save for the fact that instead of the genial Colonel, the house had as master, a grave, rather serious young man.

Victor was feeling his responsibilities, and often wished he were back in Dublin, pursuing his beloved studies, preparing for the career which he had chosen for himself. But as this was not to be, he put his shoulder to the wheel, interviewing his tenants, the steward, the gardener. His mother was a tremendous help to him, she understood the working of the estate, and had been as interested in all its details as the Colonel himself. Only for her, Victor felt he would have been lost amidst all the various business matters connected with his property. Besides this, he was a young man who took life seriously, and he worried far more over such things than his father had ever done. He was careful, too, about money. There was no fear that Victor would ever lose a thousand pounds by bad investments.

One morning, a month after his father's death, Victor was talking to Brennan, the gardener, when a boy came down the garden path in their direction. A 'boy' in local parlance, but he was evidently about twenty. Victor did not remember noticing him before, except working in the garden at a distance. Now he found himself glancing curiously at him, as he stood aside, waiting for the gardener to speak to him. Goodlooking in a way; fair-haired, grey eyes with a hint of humour; a rather bold look upon his face. Somehow, Victor did not like his appearance.

'See what this boy wants, Michael,' he said, and when a moment later, the boy had gone, walking with a debonair air, rake over his shoulder, Victor asked the gardener:

'Who is that boy, Michael? Have I seen him before?'

'He is Pat Dempsey, sir. When Joe Doyle went to America four months ago, this fellow came with a recommendation from Sir George Dare, and the Colonel took him on.'

'Is he all right?'

'Well he is, and he isn't, sir. There do be times when he is as impudent as you please, and then for that agen he will be civil enough.'

'He has no business to be impudent to you, Michael. He is working under you. Why don't you keep him in his place?'

'So I try to do, sir, but when there do be others——'

He paused, and Victor asked, quickly, 'What do you mean, Michael? He only works under you?'

'Aye, sir, that's true.'

'Well then?'

Michael was silent for a moment, and then said, rather diffidently: 'If you were to say a word to Miss Anne, sir——'

'Miss Anne? What in the world has she got to do with this boy?'

'It's like this, sir. You know that she is mortal fond of flowers—not that she knows anything about them, the cratur!—and she has a bit of ground, which I could do wid meself—not that I'm askin' for it, sir—and grows bits of plants and things like that. Well, Miss Anne has taken a notion to have Pat Dempsey to help her, and he does be weedin' and diggin' for her and wastin' his time. Of course he does have it as an excuse when I want him for some rale work. Miss Anne—wid all due respect to her—is just spoilin' him, and signs on it, he's gettin' uppish in himself. Only for that, sir, he's well enough, and knows his work.'

Victor laughed.

'Well, you speak to Pat,' he said, 'and I'll ask Miss Anne not to take up so much of his time—it's not fair to you, Michael. And now what about those grapes?'

It was not until he saw his sister at lunch that he remembered Michael's words, and smiled to himself at the notion that Anne was spoiling the garden boy. The meal was just over, and the servants had left the room, when he said, with a twinkle in his eyes: 'Look here, Anne, what's all this I hear about you spoiling

Michael's boy? He tells me that you are wasting his time getting him to work for you—wasting the ground, too, according to Michael's opinion! Don't encourage the boy to shirk his real work—you know what these fellows are!'

His sister did not reply, and turning to look at her, he was amazed to see that she had flushed scarlet. He stared at her. Surely she was not taking his words seriously.

'Don't get huffy, Anne. Of course, you can have the boy to weed and so on, whenever you want him, only don't take up too much of his time, as Michael is very busy just now and wants help.'

She answered him furiously.

'What business is it of yours if I have Pat to help me or not? Oh, of course I must not forget that you are master here now—not that you are likely to let me forget it! I suppose my garden will be taken from me next. Perhaps you would like me to pay rent for it?'

'ANNE!'

She laughed, bitterly.

'Oh, yes—you can pretend to be horrified. But I know quite well that you do not want me here——'

'Anne—hold your tongue at once!'

It was Mrs Hewdon who spoke, but her daughter turned upon her, as she had never done before.

'Yes—you, too, mother! You would like me to be gone from Ballafagh! You think I should get married—anything to get rid of me. Well, perhaps you will have your wish sooner than you expect!' Then, rising from her seat, she flung herself from the room.

'Mother—what is the matter with Anne? I meant nothing—it was only that Michael was inclined to be vexed because the boy was wasting time doing small jobs for Anne——'

'Do not let her worry you, Victor. She is exceedingly difficult, and no one knows what I have had to suffer from her. And then your poor father ruined her—she was always his favourite as you know.'

'She is—queer,' replied Victor, 'I never could quite understand Anne—one never knew what she was going to do next.'

'That is true. I wish that she would marry, my mind would be at ease about her then. She would be happier in a home of her own. She and I do not harmonise.'

'She will probably marry before long. I should not let that worry me, mother.'

There was silence for some moments. Victor was considering whether this was a favourable opportunity to broach the subject of his own marriage. He felt a bit nervous at the idea, but finally decided to risk it. As Mrs Hewdon rose from the table he said: 'Come into the garden for a little, mother—I want to talk to you.'

Always ready to be with her son, of whom, since the death of her husband, she had seemed to grow more fond, Louisa Hewdon slipped her arm through his, and strolled at his side to the Rose Garden.

A lovely spot, one of the show places of the county—the Rose Garden at Ballafagh House. The roses were in full bloom, their mingled scents all around, and there, on a stone seat, by the sunken pond, where the water lilies floated, mother and son sat down.

Victor was silent for so long that at last, Mrs Hewdon, with a glance at his serious face, asked him what it was that he wished to speak to her about? The reply when it came electrified her.

'About my own marriage, mother.'

Struck dumb, she stared at him, not comprehending. Was it possible—but no, of course not, it couldn't be—that Victor was talking of getting married?

She moistened her lips.

'What do you mean?'

'What I say, mother,' with a nervous laugh, for some premonition told him that his ordeal would be a hard one: 'I am going to be married.'

'Indeed,' in tones of ice, 'and might one inquire the name of the future mistress of Ballafagh?'

'You know her, mother. Nora Harding.'

If Louisa Hewdon had been surprised before, she was literally bereft of speech now. Victor went on talking.

'You know Nora, mother—how nice she is—such a dear! You must like her as it is, and you will soon love her. I cannot tell you all she means to me. We have loved each other ever since first we met—the day of the Garden Fête which you gave for the Nursing Association—you remember?'

But Louisa Hewdon sat motionless, an image of stone, her face expressionless, her eyes staring in front of her, seeing nothing.

'Mother—won't you speak to me? Don't look like that—please!'

Without turning her head, she replied: 'What is there for me to say? You have already arranged your own future. I will only ask you to let me know when you wish me to leave Ballafagh. Would it be inconvenient if I asked you to allow me to remain for a week from now? I have my packing. And I must make my plans. Perhaps Evelina will have me to live with her, as no doubt she will also be going.'

Victor stared at her, aghast. What was this his mother was saying?

'Mother, darling—don't speak like that! As if I would ever allow you to leave Ballafagh. Why, it is your home—will always be your home. Do you forget that Dad left you to me?'

'I do not forget, but evidently you do.'

'But surely you did not expect me to remain unmarried all my life?'

'Certainly not. But I expected you to marry a woman who was your social equal—a woman who would not disgrace your name.'

'Even you must not speak in that way of Nora. What have you against her?'

'She is of no family, and has no money. You should marry money, it would be a great help. Then this woman is older than you are. That is why she entrapped you so easily.'

'Please stop!'

Even from his mother he could not listen to such words. How could she speak like that? Entrapping him! How vulgar, how unlike his stately mother.

She made as if to rise, to leave him. He put out a detaining hand.

'Don't go yet, mother. Let us talk this thing over quietly.' Suddenly he felt stronger, more of a man. They must have it out—finish it once and for all.

'Nora and I meant to marry as soon as I was called to the Bar,' he said; 'we would have settled in Dublin, for, of course, I did not dream that Dad would die so soon. We knew that there might be some opposition to our marriage, but were sure that you and Dad would soon forgive us. And you will do so now—won't you, mother? If you really knew Nora——'

'That is enough—please, Victor! My knowledge of Nurse Harding is quite sufficient for me. I have no desire to add to it. It would be quite impossible that I could receive her as my daughter-in-law. If your mind is made up—if you are determined to marry this person—then it is best that I should leave here at once. I do not believe in putting off the evil day. I had rather go now than wait for the few months which will intervene before your marriage. I suppose it will be soon?'

'Not for some time yet, mother. Please think things over and do not think of leaving your home.'

'It would be useless.'

'But why, mother? Come now, what objection have you really to Nora beyond the mere fact that she does not belong to a county family? And as for money, you surely do not want your son to be mercenary?'

He tried to bring a smile to her lips, but she did not respond; still, when he took her hand she did not withdraw it.

'I have always loved you, mother—always. You know that I would do anything to please you.'

'Anything but the one thing I ask of you.'

'To give up Nora? I cannot do that.'

Suddenly he was dismayed to hear a sob, to see her tears falling—tears from this woman who so seldom cried, who had hardly wept when her husband had died.

'Mother—darling mother! I wish I could do this to please you. But it is impossible. I cannot—I will not—give up Nora.'

For a moment there was a silence, and Louisa Hewdon, by an effort of will, regained her self-control. Presently she spoke again, quietly, in cold level tones.

'You say I have nothing against this woman except her lack of family and money. There is, however, one grave obstacle which you seem to have overlooked. Nurse Harding is a Roman Catholic.'

'I know she is, and I wish she were not. But we can each go our own way at first, and then I thought—I hoped—that after a little while she might leave the Roman Catholic Church.'

His mother's jarring laugh, silenced him.

'Have you spoken much to her on the subject?'

'Not much.'

'Did she seem one who was likely to change her religion?'

'No, I am bound to say she did not. Rather the reverse in fact. Still——'

'Do not be a fool! The woman will never change, but she will try and make you do so. And if you have children—what about them?'

'They will be Protestants, of course, mother. You need not ask that.'

'Have you mentioned the matter to Nurse Harding?'

'No, I did not think it necessary.'

'Then ask her. And bring me her answer.'

CHAPTER V

THE PARTING OF THE WAYS

Nora Harding was just sitting down to her tea. She had been visiting a case some miles away, and was hot and tired. She would be glad of a cup of tea. As she was pouring it out, she heard the click of the gate, and footsteps which she knew well, coming up the tiny path to the door. She ran to open it.

'Victor! I am so glad! I was just having tea—I'm only back from Raheen. You will take a cup?'

He said he would, but it was only to please her; he was so worried that he would not have known what he was drinking. He watched her as she moved about, getting another cup and saucer, cutting cake. How charming she was in her uniform, her soft hair escaping in little tendrils from beneath her cap—worn with such a becoming air. He had never seen her untidy or careless about her clothes; mostly in uniform, she was always tidy as a new pin; when in mufti, she dressed plainly but well. Nothing shoddy for Nurse Harding.

When Victor saw her in her own cottage, she always appealed to him in a special way. He would often picture her as his wife, keeping house for him when they were married and living in their future home in Dublin. Not a grand place, just a house in the suburbs, but how happy they would be! Then when he got on, made his name with some *cause célèbre*, they would be able to live in better style, and Nora should have servants—every comfort. So he used to dream in the days before his father's death had so completely changed his position. More than ever, he wished that the Colonel had lived longer. That dream house in Dublin would never materialise now.

Still they would surely be quite happy at Ballafagh. He would speak to Nora now, and put matters plainly before her. She was so sensible that she would understand at once.

They chatted away during tea—at least Nora talked and Victor listened—but all the time her eyes were watching him, waiting until he should tell the real reason of his visit. He did so when tea was over, saying quietly: 'I want to talk to you, Nora, about ourselves—our future.'

'So I guessed,' she replied with a little smile; 'You have had a talk with your mother?'

'Yes. How did you know?'

'No matter. What did she say?'

He hardly knew how to begin. He hated telling her that his mother was absolutely against their marriage. Perhaps he had better tackle the religious question first.

'Nora,' he said, 'when we are married would you be willing to change your religion? It would be so much better in every way if we were both of the one way of thinking.'

She did not speak for a moment. She was thinking: 'This is your mother's doing.'

Then she said, calmly: 'No, I could never do that.'

'Why not?'

'Because I am a Catholic.'

'But Catholics change their religion sometimes.'

'Perhaps. But I am not that kind of Catholic.'

'Would you not take time and think it over—please Nora, darling? You see my mother—she is very much against us marrying—indeed she says she will leave the house if I marry you. She feels it fearfully, and you know that poor Dad left her in my charge. How could I let her go away? But I am sure that she would not object so much if you were not a Roman Catholic.'

'Probably not. I always knew how Mrs Hewdon felt about the Church. But what you ask is impossible. You do not understand, but if you were a Catholic you would know what it means to us— our Faith.'

He sighed.

'Mother thought you would feel like that. She said you would not change.'

'No—I will never change. I would rather die!'

Her eyes were shining, on her face an expression he had never seen there before. He stared at her in dismay.

'There is another matter,' he said, rather diffidently, hating to have to question her like this—'suppose—if we had children—you know, Nora, they would have to be brought up in my religion.'

The girl did not reply for some moments, and taking her hand in his, he asked: 'Would you mind that? You would understand that the Hewdons of Ballafagh must be Protestants?'

She withdrew her hand gently as she replied: 'I will have to explain my point of view to you. The Catholic Church never approves of so-called mixed marriages. She never gives them her blessing, and she lays down certain regulations and conditions which I as a Catholic would be bound to obey. If God sent us children they would have to be baptised into the Catholic Church and brought up as Catholics. Unless I had your solemn promise about this, I could not marry you.'

He did not speak and she went on, with a catch in her breath: 'Victor, my dear—I have prayed for you so! I have prayed that you might get the grace of conversion—that the wonderful gift of Faith might be yours. Won't you at least go under instruction? You know nothing about the Church, and have the usual prejudices against it. Will you do this for me?'

'No—it would be useless. I know my own mind. Surely you do not think that I have come to my age without having formed my own opinions about these matters? I am a Protestant, and will remain one. You say you cannot change your religion—neither can I.'

'But you might at least learn something about the Catholic Church——'

'I know enough,' he interrupted, 'perhaps more than enough. You will say that I am prejudiced—well, it is in my blood. Do you know the stock from whom I am sprung?'

'I know your family were originally Cromwellians.'

'Yes, the first of our race who came to Ireland was one of Cromwell's Ironsides. Do you know how we got the name— Hewdon?'

'No.'

'It appears that our first ancestor who came to Ireland was named Hugh. He probably possessed some Biblical sobriquet as well—you know how the Puritans used to call themselves by all kinds of queer titles. Anyway Hugh was this man's name, but his surname is unknown—if he ever had one. The story goes that when the English soldiers were in Larramore, he was sent, with some others to the Monastery of Raheen. You know the ruins of the old Abbey which are still there? It was a great place in those days, and the community flourishing. The Cromwellian troops attacked, slaying every soul within the wall. It was just a massacre, of course, the monks were unarmed, defenceless. It is said that this Hugh slew the Abbot with his own hands, as he stood on the altar celebrating

Mass. When word was brought to Cromwell, it is said that he cried: "Well done, Hugh! Hew them down! Smite and spare not—hew them down!" He was from that day called "Hew Down," and from that we got our name of Hewdon. To that ancestor Cromwell gave a grant of much of the Abbey lands, including the site where Ballafagh House stands now. The estate has grown smaller—it was much larger at one time. So now, Nora, that may help you to understand me better. I have the blood of that man in my veins. Do not think that I am proud of it, that I approve of the man—he was a blood-thirsty butcher——but the fact remains that I am his descendant, and I have always thought that this accounts for the very definite repugnance which I have always felt towards your Church.'

'The Colonel was not like that.'

'No. Dad was the most tolerant of men. He often used to say that it didn't matter by what road we travelled to Heaven, as long as we got there in the end. But I am different. Had I lived in earlier days, I would have been a Puritan—and a stern one.'

Silence followed save for the buzzing of a bee, the purring of the cat on the window sill. From without came the scent of Nora's flowers, the lowing of cows in the distance. Pleasant, homely sounds, carrying with them no hint of sorrow or sadness; yet within the cheery cottage there was a sense of impending tragedy, the two sitting there seemed to see the wide gulf of separation which had opened between them.

Then Victor rose from his seat, and going to Nora put his hand on her shoulder.

'You will think it over, Nora? Don't make up your mind in a hurry. We will talk about it again.'

But she rose too, and stood facing him.

'It would be no use, Victor. I can never change, and I have explained to you the teaching of the Church by which I will always be bound. As to the idea of asking me to change my Faith—it is simply unthinkable.'

'You will not do so even when I tell you what a difference it might make to my mother's attitude?'

'No.'

'Then I suppose I must give you up, Nora?'

'You must do as you think fit. I can only marry you under the conditions I have told you.'

'But they are absurd—preposterous! No Hewdon of Ballafagh was ever a Catholic—or ever must be!'

'And any child of mine must be baptised into the Catholic Church.'

'It is useless to go on like this,' he said, 'we had better leave things as they are for the present. I will have another talk with my mother.'

'What is the use? Even if she agreed to our marriage, I could not marry you under the conditions you name. Let us end it now.'

He took her in his arms and laid his cheek against hers.

'Cursed be all that keeps us apart—this sectarian bitterness—'

'Please, Victor!'

'But it is hellish—all this that comes between us! Will you let this religious bigotry destroy our whole life's happiness? Nora—what are we to do?'

'There is nothing that we can do unless you will undergo instruction.'

'I cannot.'

'Then it is goodbye.'

She moved to free herself from his arms, and he suddenly realised what the loss of her would mean to him. For he loved her indeed with an exceeding love... He had never troubled his head about women until he met her—she was the one woman for him. How dear, how sweet she was! How could he part with her? His arms tightened around her.

'Nora,' he said, 'I will do as you ask. Will you make the necessary arrangements for me?'

'Oh, Victor—my dear, my dear! How I have prayed for this! But it won't be easy for you. Your mother——'

'We will meet each difficulty as it comes. And you will help me.'

They sat talking for a while longer, and then he got up to go.

'Will you tell your mother?' she asked.

'I will say nothing definite at present. It is better not. Besides,' with a smile, 'I have only promised to learn something about the Catholic Church—as you put it! I may not become a Catholic.'

'God grant you may!'

'Well—goodnight now, my darling. I will see you tomorrow.'

He went home and told his mother that nothing definite was settled with regard to the religious question, but that he and Nora were thinking matters over.

'What is there for you to think about?' she asked: 'Nurse Harding must leave the Roman Catholic Church if she wants to marry you. Surely you explained this to her?'

'Yes. We will not discuss it now, mother. I will let you know what she says when I see her again.'

Louisa Hewdon, although still uneasy, felt pretty sure that Nurse Harding would not agree to do this. But the temptation was big; marriage to a Hewdon of Ballafagh—position, money, a change indeed for the humble District Nurse. She might marry him, believing that she could 'convert' him afterwards; probably the priests would tell her to do this. One never knew with these people. How terrible to think that Victor had got mixed up with this woman. She could only hope for the best. She could ask that Nurse Harding be transferred to another district, but on reflection, resolved not to do so. It might only precipitate things—bring matters to a crisis at once. No, better to wait and watch developments.

That night, after his mother had gone to bed, Victor sat long in his own particular room, thinking—thinking. This room had been his study and contained his books and other personal belongings; he still used it a good deal, and although the days of his studies were over for him, he often sat there alone, as he was doing now.

Presently he rose from his chair, opened the door softly—all the household were in bed—and went across the hall to the diningroom. He carried the lamp with him—there was no electricity at Ballafagh in those days—and setting it on the table, sat down opposite the portrait which was supposed to represent Hugh 'Hew Them Down'. A terrible name—and a terrible man. The face upon which his descendant now gazed was stern as a rock, cruel as a beast of prey. Whoever the artist had been, he had brought out the character of the man—delineating upon the canvas, with sure strokes of the brush, the ruthless cruelty, the fanatical bigotry, the narrow mind of this Cromwellian soldier. His dress—that of the Ironsides—accentuated it all. The eyes seemed to be alive, they had a way of following one round the room, so that Victor could remember his childish fear of the picture. The servants hated it, and none of them cared to enter the great diningroom after dark if they were alone.

Other portraits were there; more hung on the walls of the great staircase, and in the corridor above. Each Hewdon of Ballafagh, from 'Hew Them Down' himself, all through the succeeding generations, had left his portrait to posterity, and hung now upon the walls of his house. All had been strict Protestants of the Evangelical school of thought, hating the ritualists of the Church of England almost as much as Catholics—the two being nearly identical in their opinion. They had fought well for England all down the years, from the day when the first of them had sacked and murdered and tortured the 'Irishry,' down to the present day, when Colonel Hewdon had helped to carry English rule into India.

In their eyes, England meant Protestantism, and so they had fought in the ranks of William of Orange and the Elector of Hanover against the Stuart Kings. Yet many of them had been good to the land of their adoption, had been good and fair landlords according to their lights; and, in these later days, when their Puritan blood had mingled with Anglo-Norman, with French, and with that of the more tolerant English of today, the Hewdons had lost much of the bigotry, the narrowmindedness of the past. They had grown, too, to love Ireland and her people, and would have felt grossly insulted if told they were not Irish themselves.

Yet, deep within each one, the Puritan still dwelt. The spirit might be dormant—but it was there.

And now, here was the present Hewdon of Ballafagh, going against all the traditions of his family. Could he do it?

He looked up at the pictured face of the first master of Ballafagh, and he thought the eyes stared back with a sinister expression in their dark depths. Victor turned his away, and buried his face in his hands.

Could he do it?

For the love of a woman, men had done as much; had given up Faith and Fatherland—their honour, their very all. Had they ever repented, he wondered? Victor, serious and grave beyond his years, now found himself considering this question. Deep in love though he was now—and he knew what his love was to him—would he, in the years to come, regret the step he had taken? That he would ever become a Catholic from conviction he did not believe. How then, could he go through the farce of entering the Roman Church? And afterwards, as the years went by to see his children going to Mass, worse still to Confession—'Oh, God—is any woman worth that?'

Springing to his feet he began to pace the room, back and forth, back and forth, with angry strides. Hour after hour went by, yet he could come to no decision, could feel no peace; he was swayed one way by his Puritan conscience—that heritage of a long line of ancestors—warning him against doing what he contemplated; on the other side his love for Nora called to him to possess her—no matter at what cost.

The battle was not finished, the issue still undecided, when at last he went upstairs to bed. It was nearly six o'clock, and the servants would soon be moving. He must try and get a couple of hours' rest.

At breakfast his mother noticed him looking pale.

'Are you not well, Victor? You look as if you had not slept?'

'I did not sleep very well, mother. But I'm all right.'

To herself Mrs Hewdon thought—'worrying over that woman! How I wish it were settled.' Then aloud: 'Anne must have overslept herself. Hayes'—to the parlourmaid—'just see if Miss Anne is up, and tell her we are at breakfast.'

In a few moments the maid returned with a rather scared face.

'Miss Anne is not in her room, madam—but I found this note for you.'

Mrs Hewdon took the note with a puzzled expression.

'What on earth is Anne up to, now?' asked Victor in annoyed tones. Was it not enough that he should have his own worries, without Anne starting to be troublesome?

His mother gave a hasty exclamation, and glancing at her he saw that her face had become pale, her hands trembling. He motioned Hayes from the room.

'Mother—what is it?'

She handed him the note, and he read these words:

'When you get these words I shall be gone. You need not try to stop me. I have taken my own pathway, and mean to live my own life. I could not stay at Ballafagh any longer, it was stifling me. You will hear where I have gone soon enough —Anne.'

That was all: Victor turned it over in his hands as he cried: 'Where in the world can she have gone?'

'We must find out,' replied his mother. She had regained her self-possession, and told Victor to ring for Hayes and ask her to inquire if any of the household had seen Anne that morning?

In his own mind Victor was thinking that his sister had probably left the house between five and six; if it had been earlier, he would surely have heard her—although even that was not likely in a large house like Ballafagh, with several exits. Even while he wondered, Hayes returned to say that no one had seen Miss Anne that morning.

Mother and son sat facing each other across the table.

'What should we do, Victor?'

'I don't know, mother. If only we had the least idea where she had gone? Would she have gone to the Merediths, or——'

'A visit—at this hour! I do not think she has gone to friends,' replied Mrs Hewdon, 'she is far more likely to have gone to Dublin. She has some foolish notion in her head about earning her own living—taking up typing or some nonsense of that sort. And you know she has her legacy to fall back upon——'

'If you please, sir,' said Hayes, in the doorway, 'Michael would like to speak to you when it's convenient.'

'Tell him I'm busy! I can't see him now,' said Victor.

'Better see him, and then come back, and we can discuss this matter fully,' said his mother.

In the hall Michael was waiting.

'Come this way, Michael.'

Victor strode down the hall to the room at the end, where all business matters in connection with the estate were transacted, and where the tenants and others coming to see the Master on business were interviewed.

Victor threw himself into a chair, impatiently.

'Well, Michael, I'm busy this morning. What is it? Don't keep me longer than you can help.'

'No, sir.'

Still, he said no more for the moment, and Victor glancing at him a trifle curiously, thought that the man looked strangely ill at ease.

'Well—what is it?'

'It's about—Pat Dempsey, sir.'

'Oh, that boy! Is he not suitable? Well, give him notice—get rid of him. Surely you need not bother me about him.'

'He's gone, sir.'

'Gone? Since when?'

'I don't know, sir. He didn't come to his work this morning.'

'Oh, well, look out for another boy, and get a man from the town to help until you are fixed up.'

'Yes, sir.'

Yet still the man lingered, and Victor, now certain that Michael wished to say something more, exclaimed at length: 'Out with it, Michael! What do you want to say—for goodness sake let me hear it!'

Michael moistened his lips.

'I saw him this morning, sir. I was at the windy'—Michael lived in one of the lodges—'puttin' on me clothes, when I seen him comin' down the avenue. It was just upon the stroke av six o'clock.'

'Oh, I see! So he was going away then?'

'I think he was, sir. He had a bundle wid him and he was carryin' a big portmanter.'

'So he sports a portmanteau, does he?'

'It was not his, sir.'

'Not his. Do you mean to say you think the boy stole it? Is that what you are trying to get at?'

'No, sir. I don't think that—I think it belonged to Miss Anne.'

'To Miss Anne? What makes you think that?'

'Miss Anne was with him, sir.'

CHAPTER VI

1916

The big grandfather's clock in the hall of Ballafagh House had just struck nine sonorous tones. A bright April day at the end of that month with May just round the corner. Out in the gardens the daffodils were bowing and swaying in the breeze, while within doors they filled every vase and bowl. On the breakfast table they made a splash of golden colour amidst the china and silver.

We were present at a breakfast in this room fifteen years ago. Coming back now, we find changes.

At the head of the table, behind the same silver teapot, which we saw before, sits a very lovely woman. She looks about twenty-five, but is nearly ten years older. Her hair is purple black with the gloss and sheen of a raven's wing; her eyes a deep grey; mouth tender and sensitive, and her colouring exquisite. No wonder she is so lovely; she was one of the daughters of Lord Larramore, and the women of that house were always famed for their beauty.

She is now the Hon. Aileen Hewdon, mistress of Ballafagh House, and mother of the tall boy of fourteen, seated at her left.

There are two other people at the table, and we have met them before. Louisa Hewdon, now an old woman, does not hold herself so upright, stoops a little, and her hair is white. In her old seat at the end of the table, sits Miss Evelina Hewdon, thinner, more angular, plainer, than when we saw her last.

The boy is like his mother, dark, with the same glossy black hair. He has an open, fearless countenance, his eyes full of intelligence, brimming over with fun and good humour. He is Hugh Desmond, only child of his parents, and heir to Ballafagh House.

The post has just arrived, and they are engrossed in their mail; even Hugh has his letter, for Victor Hewdon, from 'somewhere in France,' has written to each member of his family.

Following the traditions of his family, Victor had joined up at the beginning of the War in 1914. He had been home twice during the past two years, and so far had escaped with only a slight flesh wound. Always grave and serious, he was quieter than ever now. He never spoke of the horrors he had seen yet his people knew instinctively that he had been through a veritable inferno. He spent each leave quietly at home, never asking to go farther than the grounds, except an odd time into Larramore. Unlike many of the men home from the Front, he did not crave for amusement, it almost seemed as if his sense of enjoyment had fled—not to return.

'The dear boy!' murmured his mother, brushing the tears from her eyes, 'I wonder how he really is? They are allowed to say so little in these letters.'

'I hope he got the last parcel of socks I sent him,' remarked Evelina; 'I took such particular care with them, but he does not say anything about them. Do you think he got them, Aileen?'

'Oh, yes—I expect he did. Anyway I am sure he has heaps of socks—all the old ladies in England, Scotland, and Wales, spend their entire days knitting socks—and a few over here, too, by all accounts.'

'Really, Aileen, you are quite flippant! How can you joke on such a serious subject?'

'Am I flippant? That's funny—I could never imagine being flippant over SOCKS! Certainly not the woollen, sensible sort!'

She spoke in an airy tone of seeming indifference, a marked contrast to that of the older women. Hugh had finished his letter and put it in his pocket.

'Mother,' he said, 'can I go on the river this morning with Paddy Flynn? He is going out in the boat and will take me. You know I have only ten more days' holiday—do let me go!'

'Very well, but be home for lunch.'

'Ah—mother—can't I take lunch with me? Mollie says she will put it up for me, and it's such a grand day, and I will bring you back some fish.'

'Well—don't be late.'

As Hugh rushed pell-mell from the room after the manner of his age, Louisa Hewdon remarked, in fretful tones:

'I do wish, Aileen, that you would not allow the boy to be so much with people of that class. It cannot be good for him.'

'Why not, mother?'

Although she addressed the elder Mrs Hewdon as 'mother,' and was always scrupulously polite to her, there was no love or friendship between them. Still, Aileen deferred to her husband's mother in many ways, and was careful not to go against her wishes.

Except when she tried to interfere in any way with Hugh. The younger woman allowed no interference whatever in the way she managed her son.

'They will teach him nothing good, only the reverse. He will hear sentiments that are bad for him; his accent will suffer—he may be taught bad language.'

'Not at all. None of the Flynns would say anything of that kind in front of Hugh. As for his accent, you know there is no danger, a child will speak the accents of his home. Besides old Tony Flynn often goes fishing with his grandson, he is a native Gaelic speaker, and you know how much I want the boy to learn the Gaelic.'

'Such perfect nonsense! Only Roman Catholics and rebels learn that frightful language. Who speaks it now? What good is it?'

'A frightful language, I think,' chipped in Evelina.

'You are welcome to your opinion, Aunt Evelina, only you seem to forget, or to be unaware of the fact, that this 'frightful' language is one of the oldest tongues in all Europe. I am quite determined that my son shall learn the Gaelic.'

In the kitchen Hugh was commandeering a liberal supply of rations.

'Put up enough for three, please Mollie, because Paddy does so like your cakes, and old Tony will be there, too.'

'And what news has the master in his letter?' asked the cook, as she cut up cake and made sandwiches.

'Oh, not much. I wonder, Mollie, did he ever kill a German with his own hands?'

'God bless us—don't be saying' them things, Master Hugh. Sure if he did itself, isn't it all the fortunes of war? He couldn't help it anyway.'

'I would like to fight. But I would like to fight for my own country—for Ireland. I don't understand why Irishmen should always have to fight for England.'

The cook and Hayes—still at Ballafagh, older, more sedate—stared at the boy. Strange words indeed, for a Hewdon of Ballafagh.

'Your Grandma would be rale vexed if she heard you talking like that, Master Hugh.'

'Yes— I know. But my mother thinks as I do.'

Delia, the young kitchen maid newly arrived at Ballafagh, laughed and said, with great daring: 'Well, be all accounts there's likely to be a war here soon—and all Irishmen will have a chance of fighting for their country if they want to do so. As for me, I think all that is just a mug's game!'

'Hold your tongue!' the cook called, angrily; 'go and get me them things from the garden, and don't be talkin' a lot of rubbish!'

But Hugh was all excitement.

'Ah, sure, not at all, Master Hugh! Don't be mindin' that girl—she's just a blatherskite—no sense in her! Here's your lunch now, and I'm puttin' up some of them cheesecakes that you like.'

When the boy had left the kitchen, the cook looked at Hayes and lifted her eyebrows expressively.

'That Delia! Wait till I get me two hands on her!'

'Where did she hear the talk?' asked Hayes.

'She's a bad one to trust. The boys should be warned.'

'Ah—leave her alone—I'll speak to her.'

Aileen Hewdon was in the garden when Hugh rushed out to find her before setting off to the river. She loved gardening and was just then consulting with the gardener over the planting of some plants. Not Michael Brennan; he had retired a few years ago, and was pensioned off. This was a younger man, devoted to his work and very keen; not so taciturn or glum as Michael, he had always a pleasant smile and cheery word.

Hugh rushed up to his mother, all excitement.

'Mother—do you know that there may be a war here before long? A war in Ireland I mean. Delia was talking about it—do you know anything?'

Aileen stared at her young son, and laughed.

'Nonsense, Hugh! Who has been telling you these fairy tales?'

'It is not a fairy tale—Delia says she knows about it. Mollie and Hayes were vexed that she told me, but I'm sure it is true.'

Aileen, happening at that instant, to glance at Tom Deery, was struck by the expression upon his face. Surprise, annoyance—and was it fear? In an instant he had dropped a mask over it, and stood impassive, seemingly indifferent.

'Do you know anything about this, Tom?' she asked.

'Is it me, ma'am? How would I know what that young Delia would be talkin' about? It's romancin' that girl does be, half her time.'

Mrs Hewdon said no more, but she did not believe Tom Deery. However, she made light of it to Hugh, and he went off on his pony to ride to the river, a few miles distant, where he was to meet Paddy Flynn.

When he arrived at the old boathouse by the riverside, no one was there. Hugh seated himself under a tree, and taking a book out of his pocket began to read. It was a *Life of Wolfe Tone*—strange reading matter for a son of Ballafagh House. Yet it was not the first book of its kind that Hugh had read; he had already devoured Mitchel's *Jail Journal*, and O'Sullivan's *Story of Ireland*, and many another book like those. Where had he got them?

There was a certain Roger Patterson, a boy some two years older than Hugh, the son of the Protestant curate at Larramore. This boy was an Irish Irelander, and he it was who had first persuaded Hugh to learn the Gaelic; he, too, it was who had taught him that the Irish were a race apart from the English, that they were a nation in themselves. Slowly but surely, the boy drank in all Roger's teaching, and when he ventured to take his mother into his confidence, found, to his amazement, that she was with him, heart and soul.

Aileen Larramore came from a race whose sons, from time to time had given their lives for Ireland. The family name was O'Beirne, and up to the time of Elizabeth of England, they had been Irish and Catholic, but the O'Beirne of that time had become a 'Queen's man,' being rewarded with the title of Lord Larramore, and a large grant of land. From that time, they had been regarded as loyal to England's rule, but now and then, in different generations, there would be found one of the name who would fight on Ireland's side, one whom his family called 'rebel'. In '98, a son of the House had been shot dead while leading a band of Mayo men into battle; in Emmet's day, a cousin had ridden to Dublin and put himself at the disposal of the ill-fated young leader, being hanged afterwards for his share in the rising; and in the Fenian rising of 1867, one of the younger sons, a student at Trinity, had joined them and narrowly escaped arrest amidst the Dublin mountains.

Yet the Head of the House, the holder of the title, was always loyal to the English Empire; never once, since Elizabeth's day, had a Lord Larramore changed his politics or his religion.

And now, the old Irish spirit had come to life again in a daughter of the name. Aileen loved Ireland with a great love; she loved the old tongue of the Gael, the old manners, the old customs. She had imbued her son with her ideals, teaching him to be proud of his Irish ancestry. She had feared that his father's blood would show itself in Hugh, that the Puritan strain would prove stronger than her own. Bit by bit she taught him all she knew about the history of her land, and the boy drank it in, eagerly, gladly, longing and waiting for the day when he, too, should ride forth to do battle for his Dark Rosaleen. But his mother had never a hope that such a day would dawn in Ireland again. She had hoped for it once, but that was before the War. During these latter days, she had no hope at all.

The spring day was warm, and Hugh sat reading by the river bank, so absorbed that he forgot for a while the non-arrival of his friends. But suddenly he remembered, and glancing at his schoolboy's watch, saw that it was noon. The Flynns were over an hour behind time. He waited another hour, and then with the appetite of a healthy boy, devoured some sandwiches and cake, and had a drink of milk.

Two o'clock, and still no sign of either Paddy Flynn or the old man. He would ride into Larramore, he might as well pass the time there now, as evidently there would be no fishing today.

He untethered the pony who had been cropping the short grass, and rode into the town of Larramore, going the selfsame road as that travelled by his Aunt Anne—of whom he had never heard— and his grandfather, on that summer's day, now fifteen years ago.

As he reached the town he could not but notice that excitement of some kind was in the air. People were standing at street corners, and shop doors, talking earnestly. As he passed the Barrack, one of the men who knew him came out and put his hand on the pony's bridle.

'Are you alone, Master Hugh?'

'Yes,' he replied, 'the Flynns were to meet me at the river, but did not turn up. What's wrong, Jim? It is not a Fair day, is it?'

Hugh knew the man well, for his younger brother worked at Ballafagh.

'No, Master Hugh, but it would be as well if you went home. The town is a bit excited—not that anywan would harm you—but I'd as lief you were at home.'

'But what is it?'

'News came down that there's a rising up in Dublin and terrible fighting going on. We don't know the rights of it yet.'

'In Dublin! A Rising! Oh—how I wish I were there!'

''Tis glad you should be to be safe here. Turn round now like a good boy and go home with yourself.'

Nothing loth now, with his wonderful news to tell, Hugh

obediently turned the pony's head towards Ballafagh. His mother and grandmother with Miss Evelina were sitting at tea in the lovely old drawingroom.

'Mother! Mother! There's a Rising up in Dublin—they're fighting! Now—wasn't Delia right? I wonder how she knew? Oh, if only I were a man to go and fight too!'

'What on earth is the boy talking about?' asked Louisa Hewdon, totally unconscious of the import of his words.

Aileen had grown suddenly pale. She spoke quietly to Hugh. 'Go upstairs, dear, and wash your face and hands—you are quite dusty.' Then to Mrs Hewdon: 'Some nonsense he has heard. Another cup of tea, Mother?'

By nightfall they knew it was not nonsense. News came slowly into Mayo during that terrible week, but it did come. There were all kinds of rumours, both true and false, and all the time the people with no newspapers, no post, little means of communication with the outside world—were on edge. Feelings ran high on both sides, the tensions was acute.

And then came the day that Aileen drove into Larramore solely to try and get more news. She saw Dr McHale at his door speaking to the District Inspector of Police. She stopped the pony trap and they came to her side.

She smiled graciously.

'What is the latest news, Mr Wilson?' she asked.

He saluted smartly.

'The best, Mrs Hewdon! Nearly all the rebels have surrendered, and there is a gun-boat in the Liffey to help us now.'

He looked delighted, charmed at being able to deliver such a piece of intelligence to the wife of Hewdon of Ballafagh.

'I see. You are sure of this?'

'Quite sure! I have received it direct from Headquarters.'

'Thank you.'

'You will come in and rest, Mrs Hewdon—you look pale. This must have been an anxious time for you, especially with Mr Hewdon away. Do come in for a little—my wife will give you a cup of tea.'

Thus the Doctor, all smiles, already opening the door of the trap. But she shook her head.

'Not today, thank you, Dr McHale—I must hurry home.'

So it was over. They had failed again. After the high hopes of the first days, the disappointment was bitter.

But more bitter still was the news brought to Ballafagh during the following days. Execution after execution; wounded men taken out to be killed; courtmartial after courtmartial, and the great pit at Arbour Hill being filled with the bodies of those who died for their Fatherland.

In the kitchen, the cook and Hayes sat crying their eyes out, the other maids were depressed and gloomy, while Tom Deery and the rest of the men went about their work with a hunted look on their faces. No one knew when he would be arrested. Only Delia went around as usual, calling out to them: 'It's a mug's game—I told you it was!'

Aileen, reading those terrible lists in the newspapers—that superb Roll of Honour which will be enshrined for ever on Irish hearts—was glad when at last the tears came, and she could weep. Hugh, standing beside her, put his arms round her.

'Mother—wait till I'm a man! I will fight for Ireland too!'

There was no question yet of his returning to his school in Dublin; he would have to wait until all was quiet again.

Louisa Hewdon, hearing Hugh speak like that, turned furiously upon her daughter-in-law.

'Aileen—you have ruined that boy! What would his father say if he could hear him? All the men of his house were loyal to England.'

'I know. But please remember that I am an O'Beirne, and we are Irish. Many a man of my house has fought for Ireland against England. Fought for Ireland—died for her.'

'And I will do the same, Mother!'

Louisa stood up, trembling with rage.

'Often have I regretted the day that you became the wife of my son,' she said, 'but never so much as now.'

Aileen turned to the boy.

'Go into the garden, dear,' she said. Then, turning to the older woman: 'It is too late to regret it now. As far as I have always understood, the marriage was mostly your doing. I believe that Victor wished to marry some one very different, but of whom you disapproved. Perhaps she might have pleased you better than I do, if you had allowed you son to marry her.'

Louisa Hewdon left the room without replying. Aileen's words had gone home, for now in her old age, she saw that she had done wrong to interfere between her son and the girl whom he had really loved. But she had been afraid of Nora Harding, of her Catholicity, of her Irish ideals. Then had come the affair of Anne, and panic-stricken, Louisa Hewdon had persuaded her son into a marriage with the youngest of Lord Larramore's lovely daughters. Victor, horrified at what his sister had done, had experienced for the moment, a queer repulsion against all Catholics, and had turned back to his old ideals, to the old Puritan traditions of his family. He had done as his mother wished. If he repented afterwards, no one knew of it.

The Rising was over; England had shown the strong hand, and the 'rebels' were put down once and for all. So it seemed to most people at that time, so little did they then dream that what they thought was the end, was only the beginning.

Aileen thought it was all over as she walked along the river bank with Hugh, one lovely day towards the end of May. She was very pale and quiet, moving listlessly as one who took little interest in life.

Old Tony Flynn, rising to his feet, as she drew near bowed low, with his charming old-fashioned courtesy.

He saluted her in the Gaelic as 'Gracious Lady,' and she smiled back at him.

'Sit down, Tony,' she said, 'and talk to me.'

'My lady,' he said, 'your heart is sad within your breast. Yet it need not be so. Those who died have not died in vain—they have sown the seed which is yet to ripen and bring forth fruit many hundredfold. Even already it is so. Listen to this—before the Rising there were but seven in the town of Larramore itself that were Republicans. Today, their number is three hundred.'

'Tony! Are you sure?'

'Sure as I am that the sun is shining overhead! Sure as I am that the Dawn has broken again in Eire. My lady—take heart again, let me see you smile.'

'Ah, Tony?' she said, smiling a little to please him, 'you do me good. I wish I could believe as you do.'

He looked at her for a moment without speaking. Then he took her slim white hand in his old gnarled one and patted it softly.

'Lady,' he said, 'you will live to see the day, although I may not.'

CHAPTER VII

ANNE DEMPSEY

Anne Dempsey was scrubbing the kitchen of No. 87 Meadow Grove. Any place less like either a meadow or a grove it would be hard to find. Meadow Grove was a narrow street of drab houses, one of those numerous byways, situated off the great highway of Whitechapel Road.

The house were small—three rooms and a kitchen, the door opened right on to the street, and there was a tiny yard at the rere. They were, however, occupied for the most part by fairly respectable working people, and although Saturday nights saw many a drunken row, and the din of screaming children seldom ceased, still there were many worse places to be found in the East End of London.

Anne, rising from her kneeling position on the brick floor, straightened herself wearily. It was a spring morning in the year 1919, and Anne was now a little over forty, but looked much nearer fifty. She wrung out her cloth with work-roughened hands and went to the sink in the scullery to get more water.

She was feeling very tired, but she had to finish the kitchen and start about preparing the early dinner. Her son and daughter were both at work, and would be in to the minute of one o'clock.

As for her husband—she would expect him when she saw him. Going presently to the back door, she paused a moment, looking over the wall which divided her yard from that of her next door neighbour. The woman was from the country—Devonshire—fretting here for her home amidst green fields, daily growing paler, more listless. She had planted a lilac tree in her back yard, and rather to her own surprise, it had grown; sickly, puny, like the little children around there, but like them too, managing to keep a hold on life. And now this year, for the first time, it had blossomed.

To Anne Dempsey, standing there this morning, there had come the scent of the lilac. She stood there, motionless, and slowly her eyes filled with tears. Seldom did she weep now, her tears had dried long ago, but the well-known perfume reached her heart, opening its floodgates. Nothing can touch the chords of memory like a remembered perfume; a sprig of lavender, a wild rose, the drifted scent from a hedge of hawthorn—these will bring back the bitter-sweet memory of half-forgotten things.

So Anne Dempsey, with the perfume of the lilac coming across the wall was no longer looking at a grimy backyard in one of London's slums, but was back in the gardens of Ballafagh. Oh—the lilac that used to grow there! Great bushes of mauve, and dark purple and white. One could get the scent before one got near them—it would drift along, delicious, heavenly, as if indeed, the angels were showering down from above the perfume of Heaven itself.

The lilac at Ballafagh. Different from the poor sickly plant next door—as different as were the people here from those sturdy men and women of the West of Ireland.

Ballafagh.

What was her home like now? Was her mother alive? And Victor—what of him?

Peeling the potatoes for dinner, she went over the past years, remembering, regretting, as she seldom allowed herself to do now.

She saw herself as a girl running away from home with Pat Dempsey, the gardener's boy. She—the daughter and sister of a Hewdon of Ballafagh! She had been mad of course—quite mad, and had found out her mistake in a very short time. They had been married in a Registry Office in London. Pat had wanted to be married also in a Catholic Church, but she had refused to agree to this. He was a careless Catholic and had allowed her to have her own way, and after a while he drifted away from the Church himself, seldom going to Mass, never to the Sacraments. But when their first child was born, it seemed that his conscience awoke, and he asked her to let the boy be baptised in the Catholic Church. Anne refused angrily, had the child baptised a Protestant, and called him George after her father. In doing this she felt as if she were flinging defiance at her family. Her son, the son too, of a labourer, he should still be called after Colonel Hewdon, his grandfather.

Pat had got work at the docks, irregular work, so that he was sometimes idle, sometimes working overtime. But although he earned good pay, he had taken to drink, and his wife knew what it was to be hungry many a time.

Then shortly before the little girl was born he had been ill, so ill with pneumonia that the doctor—knowing his habits—had given him up.

'Better get the priest for him,' he had said curtly to Anne, taking it for granted that this big Irishman with the remains of good looks was surely a Catholic.

Pat had heard and the priest had been sent for, and the sick man with the fear of death before him had made his Confession. The result was that Anne and he were married by the priest, and she had promised to have the next child baptised a Catholic and to go under instruction herself. She hardly knew why she had done this. Probably she had just taken the line of least resistance, being in poor health and tired out, miserable in body and soul.

And after all Pat had not died, he had lived, and after a short spell of good behaviour, had taken to drink again, and was now seldom sober.

The baby girl was baptised Mary, and Anne, as she had promised, went to a priest for instruction. She was received into the Church after a few months, and whatever comfort she had now, came from her religion. Yet one could hardly call her a good Catholic, certainly she was not like a convert, rather did she resemble a careless Catholic, who had always had the Faith, but never really appreciated it.

As the years went by, Anne found herself wondering was she really the Anne who once lived at Ballafagh House. She would look up from the kitchen table as they sat at meals, and suddenly visualize the breakfast room in her old home; or the great dining-room, the silver and cut glass gleaming on the polished mahogany. Then she would glance across to where her husband sat in his shirt sleeves, eating voraciously, his knife in his mouth every moment, a piece of bread sopping up the gravy on his plate—and would wonder was it not all a horrible nightmare, from which she would soon awake? But he would push his plate towards her for more food, and she knew it was reality—horrible, stark reality.

It is strange that it is the small everyday things of our daily life that mean the most to us; the tiny pinpricks of human existence are the hardest to bear. A really big trial is often easier to meet, but the ever recurring little annoyances that come to us day by day, it is these that wear down our patience—perhaps their very monotony makes them hard to bear. Anne would never forget the first meal she had with Pat Dempsey. She had never seen him at table before they were married, and she had been horrified when she had seen him putting his knife in his mouth, wiping it on his bread, pushing away his plate, wiping his mouth with the back of his hand. She had stared at him aghast, while he, totally unconscious of doing anything wrong, asked her if she was not feeling well? It was her first realisation of the tremendous difference between them.

But as the years went by, she grew indifferent, became inured to it all. It was her daily life, part of her existence, and had to be borne. Only when the children came she tried to teach them manners, tried to make them more like her people, less like their father. It was not easy. They had his example always before them in the home; they went to a Board School where they could not but acquire the Cockney tongue of their companions; later when they went to work it was the same. All their surroundings, their upbringing, were against her teachings, and after a while she gave up the attempt to train them as she wished. She could only hope that heredity might do something for them.

And heredity—that strange force of which we know so little and so much—did show at times. Mary had certain ways with her, a refinement of expression, of speech; one never heard from her lips the kind of talk which was common amongst the girls of Whitechapel. This might have been due in part to her Catholic upbringing, but it was plain to be seen that coarseness of any kind was alien to her character. George, too, used no bad language; he was coldly contemptuous of those who cursed obscenely, making every second word hideous. He was too much the student, he had read, had cultivated his mind too much, to allow himself to descend to such a level. But both spoke as Cockneys, and had the Cockney outlook upon things in general. Once or twice, when their father had been sober, he tried to tell them about Ireland, to instil into them some love and knowledge of their father's land. But he was not the right person for the task; indeed, the very fact that it was he who spoke like that, turned them against all things Irish, so that when Mary was asked to join the Gaelic League, she curtly refused. Anne, of course had been brought up in the traditions of Ballafagh, and was glad when she found that her children were not going in for any of that 'rebel nonsense'.

At intervals during those past years, she would wonder what her mother would think could she see her daughter now? See her scrubbing, washing, her hands roughened, her hair grey already, dull, straggly, uncared for; her face lined with care. Twice she had written home, once to her mother, and once to Victor. There had been an interval of two years between the letters, and both had been returned without a word. She had rightly surmised that her mother had done this. In her last letter, Anne had said with truth, that she was without a penny, having borrowed the stamp. How could her mother be so hard, so merciless? She was sure that her brother would have helped her had he known of her need. Well—she would never write to them again—would starve rather.

When the War came, she watched the papers for news of Victor, for she was certain he would join up at once. She had seen his name once, he was mentioned for bravery, and had been awarded the D.S.O. But she saw nothing more about him, and often wondered if he had come home safe, or were his bones lying under the poppies 'somewhere in France?'

Her husband had joined up in 1915, and for three blessed years Anne had peace. She got work herself in a munition factory, earning good pay, and was able to keep herself and the children in some comfort. Then the war had ended, Pat had come back, the worse in body and soul, and her misery began again. In a drunken bout, one night, he smashed up the home which she had got together while he was away, not leaving a bit of furniture undamaged, throwing china and glass out of the windows. After that Anne lost heart utterly, and although Dempsey would not do that kind of thing now—having a wholesome respect for his son—she never worried about the home, leaving Mary to keep it clean and tidy, she herself only doing what was actually necessary.

The potatoes on the fire, she set the table for dinner, in the usual rough and ready way, and put some meat on to fry. She had never learned to be a good housekeeper, and could not cook. She just muddled on somehow. Only for Mary, little comfort would have been in the house.

Her daughter entered just then. She was sixteen—a year younger than her brother. Tall, with dark hair and fine eyes, she would have been quite pretty if she had been less thin, and had had some colour in her cheeks. But she was painfully thin and pale, and she never used any 'make-up' like the other girls in the big jam factory where she worked from eight in the morning until six, with an hour for dinner. She was a devout Catholic, a good girl in every way, and although working in the midst of much that was evil, amongst girls who were frankly pagan in their outlook, Mary Dempsey went her own way, unsoiled by what was around her daily path. Her companions laughed and jeered at times, yet many of them had a queer grudging respect for this girl who was so unlike them. There were a few more girls like herself, and these kept together, while being quite civil and polite to the others.

'Hèllo—mother!' she called cheerily. 'George not in yet?'

'No—not yet. Just turn that meat in the pan while I put on the kettle.'

Mary did as she was told, and then going into the scullery washed her hands, and ran a comb through her hair, having first hung her hat and coat on a peg in the kitchen.

When she went back to the kitchen her brother was there.

Every time Anne looked at her son, she experienced a queer feeling it was her brother who stood before her. The resemblance was strong. George Dempsey had Victor's serious expression and quiet ways, he was tall and had the same thick auburn hair with the natural wave in it, his eyes too, were the same shade of dark blue. But there the likeness ended, for whereas Victor Hewdon had carried himself erect with an air of assurance, George Dempsey was stooped from working all day long in a boot factory; also instead of the healthy bronzed look of his uncle, his face was sallow, unhealthy looking. He hated his work in the factory, for he was by temperament a student, and spent every spare hour either attending evening classes, or reading books which he got from the Library. He had been baptised into the Church when he was three years old and brought up as a Catholic, but for the past year he had gone to no place of worship, openly asserting that he was done with all that kind of thing—'spiritual dope,' he called it.

'Well, mother—dinner ready?'

He was always good to his mother, giving her nearly all his wages, protecting her many a time from the violence of his father, whom he detested and regarded with contempt. He was quite decent to his sister, but regarded her as a poor, priestridden fool. He went to Hyde Park on Sunday afternoons and listened to the speakers on Rationalism and Free Thought, drinking in every poisonous word, storing them up for future argument.

'Father not in?' asked Mary, as they sat down to table.

'No.'

The girl sighed. She alone, worried about the man, prayed for him every morning at early Mass, longed to see him a sober character again. His wife had given him up long ago; his son was merely contemptuous.

But today, even as Anne spoke, they heard his key in the door, his step in the passage, and the next moment he had entered the kitchen. He threw off his hat, and flung himself into a chair. He was not working these days. Now that his son and daughter were in constant employment, Pat Dempsey only worked when he liked, and even when he did so, kept most of his money for himself. As his wife helped him to some meat, she noticed that he was in a good humour.

'Mary, me girl,' he said, 'will you come to the Pictures tonight? I'm after winnin' a bet off another fella, and can stand a treat for wance—will you come?'

'I'm sorry, father, but this is my sodality night.'

Her voice was soft, but the cockney twang very noticeable.

'Ah, no—come along wid me for wance! Don't refuse your ould Dad!'

But it was no good, Mary would not miss her sodality night.

'Well—I know it's little good askin' your lordship here?' throwing a look of dislike at his son.

'No thanks—I've no time to waste like you.'

He too, spoke like a cockney, his 'waste' sounding more like 'wyste' in the ears of his father, who hated this accent of East End London, as he hated London itself, and all that it meant.

'Of course not—a learned perfessor—no less! Well, it's a quare thing that they can't teach you to speak better.'

George flushed with angry humiliation. He knew he spoke badly, and was always trying to correct himself, but environment was too much for him.

'Well, old girl, what about yourself?'

'No—I don't want to go, thank you,' replied Anne.

'Faith then, I'll find some wan to be along wid me—I'll not go alone, you can be sure of that.'

'Could you not go, mother?' said Mary. She felt uneasy, her conscience pulling her two ways. She would have liked to go with her father, to keep him out of mischief, he would not drink too much if she were with him. But she could not miss her sodality meeting.

Anne shook her head again.

'No, I do not like those places—all smells and dirt!'

Dempsey gave a loud laugh.

'Sure I was near forgettin' that I had a lady wife——'

'Shut up!'

His son's face glared across the table at him.

'By gum, I've had enough of me lovin' family—I'll go and finish me dinner somewhere else.'

He flung out again, and the door banged loudly behind him.

CHAPTER VIII

'AND PAWNED HIS SOUL FOR THE DEVIL'S DISMAL STOCK OF RETURNS' —MANGAN

As Pat Dempsey flung himself out of the house, he felt that he was an ill-used man. He could hardly be blamed for feeling bitter. His marriage had been a terrible mistake—just as much for him as for his wife. Had he married a woman of his own class, remained in Ireland, working on the land, content with the little he had, he would probably have been a good husband, a better man. But dazzled by Anne, astonished and bewildered when he understood that she wished to be his wife, he had married her almost against his will. He had certainly done so against his better judgment, being shrewd enough to have his doubts about the success of such a match. But he had not contemplated that it would develop into a sordid tragedy.

Anne had disliked him almost from the first. The enforced intimacy of married life had torn the veil of illusion from her eyes, and instead of the handsome rough diamond—the boy with 'an air about him,' she had seen only an ignorant labourer; one too, who was either incapable of adapting himself to more cultivated surroundings, or did not want to do so.

Her legacy had soon gone; it seemed to melt, for she had not the slightest idea of the value of money, and knew nothing about housekeeping or marketing. They had soon to move into one room, a small, stuffy room, which spelt misery to Anne. Then when Pat was working they took their present house, and she had managed to pay the rent and keep the home together somehow. She had a fearful dread of lodgings in that neighbourhood.

Things had not been so bad until her husband took to drink; then she had lost heart entirely, and only for the children would not have stayed with him. When he had joined up and gone to France, she did not know herself—the comfort, the peace.

Though she knew it was a sin, there were times when she could hardly keep herself from wishing that he might never return. Yet in her heart she knew he would come back. Men who were good husbands, good fathers, might get killed or be reported as missing—but not Pat.

He came back, as she had expected, and she had no welcome for him. How could she be glad to see him? He was worse in every way, and having been medically certified as suffering from 'shell shock', had a small pension which just sufficed to keep him in drink and tobacco. She would look at him reeling home at night, and her very soul would be sick with loathing. Full of self pity, she cried to heaven for help. That her husband had any reason to complain of her conduct towards him, never crossed her mind for an instant.

Yet, on his part, drunk or sober, he sensed her attitude towards him, and hated her for it. At such moments he would remember that he had not wanted to marry her—the affair had been her doing. If she had left him alone, he would never have dreamt of such a thing. Was it for him to think of Miss Anne? Faith—it wasn't likely! No, it had all been her fault. Why couldn't she have married a gentleman of her own sort? He supposed that not one of them would have her—sure she was no great beauty anyway!

His son was another disappointment. Pat, like most Irishmen, was fond of children, and he had been delighted when he was born. But as the boy grew up, he had nothing in common with his father, and George's resemblance to his uncle, Victor Hewdon, seemed to accentuate the difference between them. When looking at his son, Pat Dempsey would see before him the 'young Master', as he remembered him at Ballafagh—just as Anne would see her brother.

He was fond of his daughter, but even she annoyed him; she was so 'pious', always making Novenas for his conversion, trying to get him to go to Mass, to the Sacraments. It was years now since he had been to Confession, he had not been to it since he was out in France. There was a Padre there—ah, well, it was no use to be thinking of those things. Far better to have a drink—nothing like a glass of something to put the heart into a man.

He had made a lucky bet on a horse the previous day, and now with the proceeds in his pocket, and two boon companions with him, he went off to 'enjoy' himself.

He was quite indignant when closing time flung him out again into the glare and noise of Whitechapel. The street was reeling before him; on every side were flaring stalls, glittering cinemas, fish and chip saloons; all the rush and noise, the drab ugliness of

London's East End. To his ears came the sounds of strident voices, raucous laughter, street cries, the roar of unceasing traffic.

And quite suddenly Pat Dempsey felt sick of it all. Drunk though he was, a desperate longing came upon him for the sight of a green field in the County Galway—for the hawthorn scented roads of Mayo. Yes—it was the springtime—he'd almost forgotten it. But sure, God in Heaven! you'd never know it was the spring here. Maudlin tears rose to his eyes, and turning to the man at his side, he gave him his opinion of London, in decidedly lurid terms. The man, a cheery little Cockney, laughed. He was fairly sober, and did not mind the ravings of this big Irishman. But the laugh set fire to Pat's brain; he saw red, as he had not seen it for many years, and with an oath, shot out a great fist to fell the other to the ground.

Had the blow carried, the smaller man would have been badly hurt, but Pat slipped as he lurched forward and it was he who fell. Fell and struck his head against the kerbstone, and so lay still. A crowd collected in a moment, the inevitable policeman appeared, and Dempsey was carried across the road to the London hospital. 'Concussion. Alcoholic, too. Bad look-out for him. Any papers or means of identification?'

Thus the House Surgeon to the Ward Sister.

They found an envelope with his name and address, and sent for his wife. Meadow Grove Terrace was quite close to the hospital, and Anne arrived in a few minutes. Mary was with her. George had been out attending some meeting, and they did not know where to find him.

'This way,' said the night nurse, and presently Anne was gazing down at a quiet form in a neat hospital bed. Her husband lay there in a state of coma, unconscious of his surroundings, breathing stertorously.

Anne looked at the nurse.

'Is he very ill?' she asked.

'Yes, he has concussion. He fell in the street, and his head struck the curb. He is not in a healthy condition, and that is against him, and then when he fell he was——'

She hesitated. There was something about Anne which made her seem different to the majority of women who came to see their husbands in the hospital—at least those who came to see the 'drunks'. She answered the nurse quietly now. 'I know—he was drunk.'

'Has he had the priest?' asked Mary. 'He is a Catholic.'

'I will ring for him at once,' replied the nurse.

The priest arrived within fifteen minutes, a middle-aged Irishman with a knowledge of human nature such as only the Whitechapel slums can give one. He spoke a few words to the nurse, and then as she was putting the screens round the bed, turned to Anne. 'You are his wife?' he asked, his keen eyes glancing curiously at this quiet, self-possessed woman.

'Yes, Father.' Then she continued, as if speaking of some stranger; 'he has not been to the Sacraments for years.'

'Oh, Father—can you do anything for him?' asked Mary. 'Poor Dad! And I have prayed so hard for him, and now——'

'Kneel down and pray now,' replied the priest.

He went behind the screen and those outside could hear his voice murmuring prayers. After a while he came out and spoke to them.

'I have done what I could,' he said, 'but he is quite unconscious. It is improbable that he will regain consciousness before the end, but he may do so. I will be at hand if I am wanted.'

Wearily the wife and daughter watched beside the dying man. The nurse told them they could stay, and left the screen round the bed—ominous sign in a hospital ward.

The roar of traffic came, muffled yet distinct, from the street without; inside the ward patients woke and asked for drinks, or moaned in pain. The House Surgeon paid his nightly visit, and soon after came the Night Sister, stopping by the bed to speak to Anne.

'That concussion—the alcoholic who came in tonight—seems bad,' she said later to the nurse. 'Another Irishman, so I suppose we will have the usual scene with the relatives when he is dead.'

'I don't think so, Sister. His wife is very quiet, she speaks just like a lady—I cannot understand it. The daughter is quite different. I think they will be all right and not make a fuss.'

'Well, I hope so, Nurse! These Irish are generally troublesome— and we get such a number of them.'

So said the Night Sister, going off to her other wards.

Towards midnight, George came in. A message had been left at the house for him, and coming in late from his meeting he had come straight to the hospital. He sat down on the opposite side of the bed without speaking. His sister was kneeling in prayer, his mother sitting upright, staring in front of her, seeing nothing.

Or did she see something? A picture, perchance, of the garden at Ballafagh on a morning in June; of a girl weeding a flower bed, and lifting her head to see Pat Dempsey, the gardener's boy coming towards her. He was such a goodlooking boy—with such a way with him! And she liked the way his hair grew, and the merry glint in his blue eyes. So different from Victor with his serious expression, his grave outlook upon life; and from her cold and stately mother. It would be an adventure—a real adventure—to run away with Pat! She was so sick and tired of the monotony, the sameness of her life at Ballafagh—she would leave it and go out into the world.

She had done so—and now this! A drunken hulk dying in a hospital ward; a son and daughter, ill educated, common of speech and manner; a house in a drab street in Whitechapel.

For several hours they kept vigil, and then, just as the dawn of the spring morning was breaking over grimy Whitechapel, Patrick Dempsey opened his eyes and saw his wife.

'Why—Miss Anne!' he said.

She caught her breath, and took in her warm clasp, the poor hand, already cold, that was groping along the bed. He turned towards the window, where the light was breaking.

'Faith, the sun is risin' over the hills beyant Larramore,' he whispered. ''Tis a grand mornin'—so it is! Thank God, I can see the green fields again!'

And so died.

• • •

It was nearly three years after the death of her husband, and Anne Dempsey was waiting one evening for her son to come home to tea.

She was still in Meadow Grove Terrace, but the house was better furnished, more comfortable in every way. George had risen to be foreman in his factory; steady, intelligent, keen, he was not only a good workman, but also a good son. Mary had married a year ago, when she was only seventeen; her husband was a man of the working class, a typical Cockney in manner and accent, yet with some Irish blood in his veins, and a good Catholic. They seemed happy, yet to Anne it had been another sorrow. She could never forget that Mary was, on her mother's side, a Hewdon. To Mary and her brother all such considerations as family and pedigree were simply worn out shibboleths, of no account in the present day world.

Yet they resembled the Hewdons in many ways. George, especially, was so like, yet so unlike, his uncle Victor. The same grave manner, the same serious outlook upon the world—but how different the outlook. Those things which were of importance to Victor Hewdon, counted for less than nothing to his nephew, the ideals, the traditions which were dear as life to him, would be regarded with contemptuous amusement by George Dempsey. On the other hand, all the things that mattered to George would have been anathema to Victor.

Anne, looking at her son sometimes, would wonder what he would make of his life? Or, rather, what would Life make of him? He was so cocksure of himself now, all the arrogance of Youth was his; he meant to 'make good' as he would say, although he quite realised some of his disadvantages. He was touchy about his Cockney accent; he knew that the education which he had obtained from the Board School, followed by self study from the books at the Free Library, attendance at night classes, and so on, was good enough in its way, but that it was also inadequate. He wanted to travel, to see other countries, other peoples, and he determined that he would do so some day.

He was very good to his mother of whom he was extremely fond. They had little in common, yet seldom disagreed—except on the question of religion. Of late, Anne had been attending better to her religious duties, and her son's attitude towards the Church—or any form of Christianity was now her greatest sorrow. Yet when she ventured to say a word on the subject, he would always reply in the same way.

'It is useless to discuss these questions, mother. I do not believe in Christianity—save so far as it represents the teachings of an idealist—and for the churches of today, let them be Roman, Anglican, or Nonconformist, I have the greatest contempt. They are all the same, temples in which the rich may assemble for so-called worship—but of no use for the poor.'

Anne knew that he often spoke at meetings where the Communist crowd gathered. She feared that he would get into trouble, and was on tenterhooks when he was out late. His whole heart and soul—although he did not believe that he possessed the latter—were in this work; that will o' the wisp ideal, the Equality of Man, was his dream, and for it he studied and worked, his one aim, the uplifting of the masses, the abolition of

Capitalists, the establishment of a government on Soviet lines in England.

He worked so hard for his ideals that his mother had noticed lately how worn and tired he looked. But in vain she begged him to take thinks easier. Such advice only angered him.

'This is not time for idling, for taking our ease. We must carry the Red Flag to victory!'

This evening, coming in to his tea at half-past six, he seemed in great spirits.

'Mother,' he cried, as he washed his face and hands in the scullery—she could never get him to go upstairs for these ablutions, for he would say that he was a workingman, and wanted no nonsense—'Mother—how would you like to go back and live in Ireland?'

She nearly dropped the teapot—her hand shook so terribly. Back to Ireland—back after twenty-one years! Could she bear it? 'To Ireland?' she repeated, faintly.

'Yes—to Ireland.'

He came from the scullery and put his arms round her, as he went on: 'From all accounts that old country wants waking up badly, and now that they have finished fighting and the Treaty is in force—now is the time to open their eyes to other things.'

'But, George, there is a lot of unrest there still.'

'Oh, rot! That's nothing! They have really nothing to complain about now. I mean, of course, with regard to their relations with England. But in other ways they are hopelessly behind the times, and I have been asked to go there as Organiser.'

'As organiser for what?'

'Oh—just to form a sort of Trade Union on a large scale.' She looked at him searchingly.

'They have their own Trade Unions, I expect,' she said. 'Why should you go over there?'

'It will be a good job, and I will be well paid. I will have to give up my work in the factory, of course.'

'But, George—are you wise? You have a good position here and this—this organising business may not last.'

'It will last all right, mother, and be an extremely fine opening for me. You will like to go back there?'

'No—I do not think so.'

'But you will come—I will want you to look after me! What would I ever do without you, mother dear?'

'You will marry some day, and then you will not want me.'

'No—I am married to the Cause,' he replied, gravely.

She sighed, wondering as she often had done before, what really was this Cause, of which he so often spoke. She had but the vaguest notion about Communism, or those things for which it stood.

He stopped and kissed her.

'You will come with me?'

'Yes—if you wish it,' she replied.

'That's right! I mean to wake up sleepy Ireland, mother! I mean to make the poor fools throw off those shackles with which ignorance and religion have bound them! They are for ever talking about Faith and Fatherland—patriotism—all that out-of-date stuff. I'll teach them the Brotherhood of Man—I'll bring them under the Red Flag—show them how blind they have been, waken them up to what is going on in the world of today. It is a great work waiting for some one—and I mean to be that one!'

His mother gave him a pitying glance.

'Your tea is ready, dear,' she said.

CHAPTER IX

'TWENTY GOLDEN YEARS AGO'

Nora Harding, as her latch key opened the door of No. 65 George Square, was aware of luggage stacked in the hall.

'The new tenants have arrived,' she thought, and with a casual glance at the trunks and other impedimenta, proceeded upstairs to the third landing where she shared a flat with Rose O'Daly.

It was only ten o'clock and her friend was not in, probably would not be home till eleven or twelve; she was a journalist and her hours uncertain. Nora was tired. She had been working in the Child Welfare Clinic all morning, and in the afternoon visiting her mothers in the district where she worked, toiling up and down many flights of tenement stairs; after her tea she had gone to her Cumann na mBan meeting, and given a lecture on First Aid, with a practical demonstration on bandaging, and the application of a tourniquet. A long day and a busy one. Nora gave a sigh of relief that it was over, and that her bed and a hot bath awaited her.

'I will go to bed early,' she thought, 'and perhaps I may be asleep before Rose comes in. She will keep me talking so late. Oh—these young people!'

Nora Harding was now forty-five. On the whole, the years had dealt lightly with her; there were threads of silver amidst her thick hair, her figure was stouter, but she retained that indefinable air of eternal youth, which stays with the man or woman whose heart is young.

She made herself a cup of cocoa, turned on the geyser for a hot bath. The flat consisted of one living room, a kitchenette, two bedrooms and a bathroom. It was situated in one of the old squares on the north side of Dublin.

Nora was just falling asleep when she heard Rose come in. Her hopes that the other might go to bed without disturbing her were vain. A musical voice called: 'Where are you, Nora? Not in bed already?' and the bedroom door flew open to show Rose standing on the threshold.

'You lazy thing! Going off to bed before I got home—and I told you I wouldn't be late.'

'Oh—I don't mind that kind of talk! Besides I was so tired.'

But even as she spoke, Nora smiled at the girl of whom she was very fond.

Rose O'Daly was nineteen; slight and boyish in figure, she had small hands and feet, and curly hair, worn short. Her mother was a native of the south of France, and Rose resembled her in many ways, being dark complexioned, and having foreign gestures and mannerisms. Her parents were in Paris, and there Rose had lived up to a year ago, when coming on a visit to an aunt in Dublin, she had suddenly made up her mind to remain for a while in her father's country. He was a journalist, and his daughter followed the same profession, being now attached to one of the Dublin papers, correspondent to a Paris journal, and Dublin correspondent to several provincial weeklies. Clever, quick, almost brilliant in ways, she was making a success of her chosen career.

She had met Nora Harding at a big political meeting, had got into conversation with the elder woman, and found her most interesting. They had met several times after that, and when Rose happened to mention that she was looking for rooms, or part of a flat—her aunt having objected to her late hours and general Bohemian style of living—Nora told her that she had a flat in George Square and that the friend who had shared it with her had just got married and left.

'If you like to come for a while, and see how you like it, you can do so,' she said. 'You need not stay if it does not suit.'

The girl had come, been delighted with the flat, and the two got on extremely well together. Nora might have been the girl's mother, and at times gave her some motherly advice. Rose laughed at it, but there were times when she followed it too.

'Where have you been?' asked Nora.

Rose came and sat down on the bed.

'At Mrs O'Brien's—one of her "social evenings", you know the kind? She wanted to appear in print—hence my invitation!'

'You did not stay long.'

'No—could not stick it! Said I had a headache and came away. Listen, Nora, I heard two men talking—they were saying there would be trouble in Ireland soon. What did they mean?'

Nora was silent for a moment, then she replied;

'I cannot tell you anything, Rose. If trouble is coming—you will know it soon enough.'

'Oh—come!—You might tell *me!* If I promise to keep it a secret—will you tell me?'

Nora shook her head.

'It is no good asking me. I can tell you nothing.'

'Oh—well! If that's the way of it!——'

Rose shrugged her shoulders resignedly, but she was disappointed. A born journalist, her instinct for good 'copy' was always to the fore, and she had seen herself sending a big *coup* about coming events to her father in Paris. However, she knew of old, that it was useless to ask Nora about such matters, and so bowed gracefully to the inevitable.

'The new people, who have taken the flat overhead, have arrived,' she then announced.

'Yes—I saw their luggage when I was coming in.'

'Did you see them?'

'No—but Mrs Walsh told me yesterday that they were a mother and son.'

'I saw the son just now. He is very handsome—but his manner—his accent! Too queer for anything!'

Nora laughed.

'His English accent, of course. You must remember, Rose, that you have never lived in England, and accent makes a tremendous difference. I believe he comes from London—he may speak like a Cockney. Now do let me get to sleep—I am tired.'

It was on the following evening that Nora saw the new arrivals. She came in at tea-time and just caught a glimpse of the mother who was on her way upstairs, but the son was standing in the hall, glancing through some letters in his hand. His back was towards Nora who was about to pass him when he turned round and suddenly faced her. She stared at him, dazed, speechless, unable to move. So pale did she become, that she startled him. Had he frightened her? But how?

'I beg your pardon,' he said.

Still she continued to stare at him, not moving. He might have been a ghost, standing there in the old Georgian hall.

'Can I do anything for you?' he asked. What kind of a woman was this? What had he done to upset her like that?

Then Nora pulled herself together. The accent in which he spoke made her realise her mistake.

'I am sorry—I thought you were someone else.' She smiled faintly as she spoke. 'You are the new tenant, I think?'

'Yes—we came yesterday. That was my mother who went upstairs just now.'

'I see. Would you mind telling me your name.'

'I am George Dempsey.'

'Thank you. Good evening.'

Her legs still shaking, Nora found herself in her own flat, and threw herself into a chair. Dempsey. An Irish name, of course, but what a terrible Cockney accent. And the resemblance. Dear God!— the resemblance! She had been so sure—so absolutely sure for the moment—that there, in the flesh before her, had stood Victor Hewdon—the Victor whom she had not seen for twenty years. It was only when she remembered those twenty years that realisation came.

'What a fool I am! Why, Victor is a middle-aged man now—and that other is but a boy! Yet he is just as Victor was—then!'

The name of Dempsey had conveyed nothing to her; if she had ever heard the name of the 'gardener's boy', with whom Anne Hewdon had run away, it had long ago escaped her memory.

But there were other things which she had not forgotten—which she would never forget.

Sitting there, in the old Dublin square, the traffic coming to her ears in a muffled roar, she was back again in Larramore; back in the Nurse's Cottage, where the roses used to climb all over the porch, where the sun rose over the hills of Mayo every morning. The roses had been all in bloom on that summer night when she had received the letter from Victor, telling her that they must part—that all must be over between them. After all these years, she knew the letter, word for word, but now, rising from her seat, she went to her bureau, unlocked it, and from a hidden drawer, took out a packet of letters, tied with faded blue ribbon—the same letters which the Nora Harding of twenty years ago used to read sitting up in bed, read them over and over again, put them under her pillow with a kiss, and then go to sleep to dream of the writer. No wonder that the Nora Harding of forty-five, let fall a few tears at the remembrance of that girl who had lived and loved in Larramore so many years ago.

Two days before Victor had written her that last letter, he had left her with his promise to go under instruction in the Catholic

Faith. He had told her that he loved her too much to give her up, that even in spite of his mother's opposition—and they both knew how powerful that could be—he would still marry her. How happy she had been that night! How she had thanked God again and again for the gift of Victor's love, praying too, that he might be a convert in very earnest. She had been too happy—she knew that afterwards.

The next day, going her rounds, she had heard the news as it flew from house to house. Miss Anne, up at the Big House, had run away with the gardener's boy—gone to Dublin, or maybe to England. Glory be to God! Who ever heard of the like? She had pooh-poohed the rumour, but as the day wore on, and the details grew more circumstantial, she had begun to wonder could it be true? She had not met Anne Hewdon often, and the few times on which they had come in contact, Nora had caught the impression of a discontented, bored girl, who would have been happier had she been one of a poor family, obliged to earn her own living. But to do this mad thing! Was it possible? Surely Victor would come that evening, and tell her the truth about the whole matter. But the evening passed and he did not come. Neither did she see him all the next day, but about eight o'clock the click of her gate was heard, and she sprang up to welcome him. The disappointment had been great. It was only a man from Ballafagh with a letter for her.

'From the young Master—no, there's no answer, Nurse.'

She had sat down in the pleasant room to read it, and being one of those psychic individuals who can sense a calamity as it draws near, Nora Harding had known, by the very touch of the envelope, that it contained bad tidings. What could they be? Too soon she had known, and now twenty years afterwards, she opened the letter again, spreading out the faded lines before her, reading once more the words, which she had thought had broken her heart that summer evening so long ago.

'Beloved—I may call you that for the last time. By now you will have heard about my sister—of the fearful disgrace which she has brought upon our name. My dear mother is broken-hearted, I do not think she will ever be the same again. From now on, she must be my first care. She has asked me not to marry you—not to marry a Roman Catholic; she feels this doubly now on account of Anne, and I must confess that I think she is right. I feel that I could not marry a Roman Catholic now. I must marry one of my own creed.

Do not think that I love you less. No, my dearest, I want you to know that no other woman will ever take your place in my heart or life. If I marry in the future, it will be for some other reason besides love. But, as I have said, my mother must now be my first consideration, my duty is with her who has lost husband and daughter in such a short space. I cannot—I will not—add to her sorrow.

'Farewell, my beloved. Forget me—I am not worthy of you.

Victor.'

If he married, it would not be for love. Yet within the year he had married the youngest and loveliest of Lord Larramore's daughters. His mother had schemed for the match, and common report said that the young couple had little say in the matter; still both were young, she so lovely, he good-looking, manly—what more could either want? Surely they had grown to love one another before long.

Nora remembered how the night she had received the letter, she had sat, dazed, stupid, not understanding, not comprehending its import. About eleven she had risen from her chair meaning to make a cup of tea, but even as she was putting the tea in the pot, sudden realisation came to her; she knew that never more would she make tea for Victor, never again would his step sound upon the path, the click of the gate send her flying to meet him. With a stifled cry, she flung the caddy from her, and throwing herself full length on the floor, had so remained until the dawn. Misery unutterable had swept over her; she thought that she could not—simply could not—bear this thing which had come upon her. Only pride kept her from writing to him, from grovelling in the dust at his feet, craving for one more meeting, asking him not to leave her like that—to see her again—to kiss her farewell. But pride, commonsense, the consolations of her faith, her old self-control, the discipline learned in the hospital ward—all had come to her aid. She wrote and got a transfer to another part of the country where she stayed for fifteen years, and then had been appointed to do Public Health work in Dublin city.

During the twenty years which had passed since she left Larramore, other men had come into her life, had wished to marry her, but Nora remained single. She could not put another man in Victor's place; his letters might be old, faded like the rose leaves of yesterday, but his memory lived in her heart, fresh, fragrant, as the roses that bloomed each summer in Larramore.

It had been a long time before she recovered from the blow; it was only gradually that the sorrow grew less, the pain became numbed. Not often now did she think of her old love story. For long periods at a time, it would not cross her mind, and then—a passing face in the street, a turn of the head, some stranger who bore a resemblance to the man whom she had loved—and it would all come back to her again.

> *'So far apart our pathways since*
> *that summer eve have been,*
> *Such joys have been lost,*
> *Such sweet dreams crossed,*
> *So much we have done and seen.*
> *Perhaps we two shall never walk*
> *through a sunset hour again,*
> *But I can recall each step of the way:*
> *is the memory joy or pain?'*

Of late her interest in her work on the district, and her activities in the Cumann na mBan had absorbed her thoughts. Therefore, the shock when she encountered George Dempsey had been all the greater.

One morning, a week later, Anne Dempsey was standing in the hall, glancing through some letters which had just come by the post. As was the custom at No. 65 George Square, the maid had left them on the hall table for the tenants to look through and select their own. There was a footstep on the stair, and a pleasant voice asked: 'I wonder is there a letter for me—Nora Harding?'

As Nora spoke she glanced at Anne, but without any recognition. It would indeed have been hard for her to recognise in this elderly woman, grey-haired, with a face worn and lined, the young Anne Hewdon whom she had met but a few times, twenty years ago.

But Anne knew Nora. She remembered the name of the District Nurse with whom her brother had been so infatuated; she could hardly forget her mother's observations at that time, and her fear that Victor would marry the girl. That had not happened anyway, for undoubtedly this was the woman; allowing for the changes made by the years, it was the same Nora Harding whom she remembered in the Nurse's Cottage at Larramore.

So what she had dreaded when she came to Ireland, had come to pass; she had been barely a week in Dublin, and here was a voice from the past—someone who might recognise her.

Her relief was great when she saw that Nora did not know her.

On her part, Nora glanced through the letters, took up two, and with a courteous 'good morning' went upstairs.

The manner of the new tenant puzzled her a little. She had seemed put out, almost annoyed, when spoken to. Nora wondered why? Also there had been something vaguely familiar about the woman. Had she met her before? Nora did not think so. How could she have done so when these people had only arrived from London a week ago, and the caretaker had said that they had always lived in England.

'My imagination, I suppose!' she thought; 'and perhaps the queer likeness that the boy has to Victor, may have caused me to think all sorts of nonsense.'

At the breakfast table Anne said to her son:

'I should like to leave here, George—I don't like this flat.'

He stared at her in surprise.

'But you seemed so pleased with it, mother! What has happened to make you change your mind?'

'I would like to go somewhere else.'

George frowned.

'But we are just settled in. Really, mother, it would be a nuisance to move so soon! And I am so busy now, just getting into the hang of things in this queer city. Do try and stay for a while.'

So as she could not give any reason for wanting to leave, unless she told him the truth—and that she did not want to do—Anne had to remain at 65 George Square. However, she was careful to avoid the other tenants of the big house—especially the two who lived in the flat beneath her own.

CHAPTER X

NOT WANTED

The stout man looked up from the letter in his hand. 'Your are Comrade Dempsey?' he said. 'Glad to meet you. Comrade Doyle will take you in hand for tonight. Here—Jim!'

A small man with a pale, unhealthy face, came across the room.

'This is Comrade Dempsey, from London—he has been sent from H.Q. to help us here. You might take him round tonight.'

James Doyle glanced sourly at George. He showed plainly that he had no particular wish for his company; however, he just nodded, and telling him that he would be back in a few moments, disappeared into an inner room, leaving George to wait his pleasure.

Sitting down on a bench, George surveyed the room. It was large, the bare boards not too clean; there were a few chairs and some benches round the wall; some notices were pinned to a board, and a big deal table was littered with literature of the usual propaganda type. The two windows were grimy with dirt, the grate full of rubbish. The one object in the room which could give any pleasure to the eye was the marble mantelpiece, of beautiful design and workmanship. The house had once been the abode of fashionable Georgian society in the eighteenth century. Now it was let in tenements, with the exception of the two 'drawing-rooms' which were let to the organisation to which George belonged, and for whom he was now a paid official.

It was about seven o'clock on a warm May evening. From the street without came the noise of children, as they shouted and sang, playing the eternal games of childhood in the filthy gutter with as much enjoyment as if they were their rich brothers and sisters, playing in beautiful gardens; on the doorsteps, slovenly women sat and gossiped; the ice cream man was doing a roaring trade from any youngster with a half-penny for a 'slider'; and in the hallway of No. 8—where George was waiting—a starved kitten was gnawing at the head of a putrid cod-fish—nearly as big as itself.

All was sordid, drab. To George all was familiar, simply reminding him of the East End of London. He looked forward to the day when Communism should be triumphant; Capitalism and all its evils demolished, and the downtrodden masses, free, uplifted, should inhabit ideal dwellings with roof-gardens. Every man equal, no private hoarding allowed, no money extorted in the name of religion.

He ventured on a few remarks of this kind to James Doyle as they set off on their round, but to his surprise they were not very well received.

'Lookit here—you're English, and you don't understand the people here. Better keep yer mouth shut till you know more!'

Their first visit was to a house a few streets away. In a dirty room— the 'two pair back'—a man sat at the open window smoking a fag; a woman was nursing a baby on her lap, and two other children were playing on the floor.

'Well, Brennan—how are you tonight?' asked Doyle.

The man looked up, grunted and then spat, but the woman replied in a whining tone: 'Ah, he's only middlin', sir. He does have a cough terrible bad be times.'

'This man was shell shocked during the war,' explained Doyle; 'he has a small pension, but not enough to live on.'

'Not enough? I should think it wasn't!' said the man. 'What's twelve and six a week to a man that's not fit for work? Eh? That's what I ask yer!'

'It is a shame indeed!' cried George. 'But don't despair—all that will soon be changed. The whole world is crying out for a change, and we are going to make it.'

The man looked at him curiously, as did the woman. His Cockney accent, unfamiliar in their ears, caused the man to inquire.

'Ye're from England, I'm thinkin?'

'Yes.'

'Well, we don't want you over here. Why not keep to yer own people, and lave us alone?'

'Comrade Dempsey is really Irish,' interposed Doyle, 'but he has been away for a long time.'

'To me,' said George, clearing his throat for one of his pet orations, 'Nationality is nothing—of no account. My parents were Irish, and I was born in England. But the Brotherhood of Man is an International ideal—'

He spoke for some time, until he realised that Doyle was telling him it was time to go, that they had others to see that evening. The woman, frankly bored, had put the child to bed, and started to clear away the remains of a nondescript meal. The man smoked, spat, and listened with a sort of contemptuous amusement.

'I've heard that sort of talk before,' he remarked as they stood up to go, 'but it doesn't fill an empty belly! Why, the St Vincent's—even if they do jaw about goin' to yer religious juties and such like—well they leaves yer a food ticket after all, but the like of yous——'

He spat finally and conclusively.

'This is really dreadful,' said George, when they got outside the door; 'these people have not the slightest idea of our aims or ideals.'

'So I told you. Now perhaps you would like to see a different type—the priest-ridden kind?'

'Certainly. I want to see them all.'

'The O'Briens live next door—in the drawingroom. We may not get a cordial reception—but we will try.'

A young woman opened to their knock—a very different person from the sloven next door. This was a clean, tidy woman, with a pleasant, contented expression on her pretty face. But the expression changed when she saw her visitors.

'Didn't I tell you, the last time you were here, that we did not want you to call again?' she asked Doyle.

'This is a worker from London,' he replied, 'he wants to see your husband for a moment on business.'

She turned her head.

'Pat! Someone wants you!'

From an inner room there came a young man of about six and twenty. He had been mending a boot which he held in his hand, and the glance with which he favoured his visitors held no welcome.

'Well—what is it?' he asked, curtly. 'What do you want now? Didn't you understand what the wife told you last time?'

George smiled.

'If you would allow me to speak to you for a few moments——'

The man looked at him, curiously. 'Come in,' he said then, 'but don't be long—I've work to do.'

George took a lightning survey of the clean, comfortable room; the dresser with its load of shining crockery; the chairs scrubbed white, the linoleum polished; the religious pictures on the walls; the lamp burning before a statue of the Sacred Heart.

He started to speak then, going over the old ground of the Brotherhood of Man, the joys of the ideal Communist state, the abolition of all Capitalism, the emancipation of the masses, painting in glowing colours the day when all men should be equal.

When he ceased, Pat Hegarty gave a short laugh.

'Your talk may be very well for idle fellows, who want to do no work and get big pay. As for meself, I am a house painter by trade, and I do an honest day's work for an honest day's pay. What I earn is my own, and if you think I would allow some idle good-for-nothing, like the fella you are so friendly with next door, to have a share in my earnings—you are much mistaken. What I earn with my hands, I mean to keep and spend as I like. If you want me real opinion, I think your talk is all balderdash. And now, if you don't mind, I've a job I want to finish. Tomorrow is Sunday, and I want these boots for early Mass.'

'Mass! Superstition! That is the cause of all your misery in this country. You allow yourselves to be priest-ridden——'

But the young man had reached the door in two strides.

'Out you go—or do you want me to throw you out?'

Crestfallen, angry, George found himself stumbling down the tenement stairs.

'I told you that you did not understand our people,' remarked Doyle, 'if you talk like that, you will do far more harm than good—and mind now, I'm warning you!'

In the next house, the door was slapped in their face, and in only one room did they get a hearing after that. It was occupied by an old man, quite deaf, and his daughter. As soon as they discovered that these people were not the St Vincent's gentlemen, they had no further use for them.

At the last house in the street the drawingroom door was opened to their knock by a tall young man, who glanced at them sharply.

'Not for us, Dan,' cried a voice from within the room, and before George could speak a word the door was shut in his face.

'Those are some of the I.R.A., I expect,' remarked Doyle, 'I know they meet somewhere here. And now we may as well knock off for tonight. Mebbe next time, we will have better luck—altho' I don't believe that the like of you will ever be any good over here—better for you to have stayed on the other side.'

He spoke in dull tones, as one little interested, and George thought how little suited this man seemed for the work of organisation. The people too—so totally different from those in England; so apathetic, indifferent to those matters which to George seemed the burning questions of the hour.

It was a decidedly crestfallen and downhearted young man who arrived at the house in George Square about half-past ten that night. In the hall, he saw the pretty girl whom he had encountered on the night of his arrival. She was standing by the table glancing at a paper in her hand, and on seeing him, smiled and nodded. He smiled back rather shyly.

'How do you like Dublin?' she asked.

'Not much.'

'Not much? But why?'

'Oh—I don't know. I cannot understand the people—they seem queer.'

'Different from those to whom you have been accustomed, I suppose?'

'Very different.'

'Perhaps you have only met a certain type of Dubliner? You know there are all kinds amongst us.'

Then as they went upstairs together, she said: 'Come in and have a cup of coffee—we are just going to have our supper.'

Opening the door of the living-room, she called out: 'Here is Mr Dempsey—from the flat overhead, you know. I have asked him in for a little talk and some coffee.'

Nora, quite used to Rose's ways, extended a welcoming hand.

'Come in,' she said, 'please do not feel a stranger.'

Over coffee and a sandwich, George told them a little of his experiences that evening. They could not understand his conversation, did not grasp what he meant, for he spoke of his social work, and they took him at first to be a Visitor for the Society of St Vincent de Paul, or some similar organisation. Then suddenly, a chance word or two, opened Nora's eyes, and she sat aghast; but as he continued talking she rather rudely began to laugh. He looked at her in surprise. He had said nothing funny—as far as he knew.

'Oh, please forgive me!' she said. 'But if you mean that you are here to teach Communistic doctrines—well, you will never get anywhere with that kind of thing in Ireland.'

'But there are some Communists in Dublin.'

'Yes—just a handful, and they are mostly foreigners. You see,' she continued, more seriously, 'I am a Welfare worker, and know the poor of the city, as only one who has free access to their homes can know them. You will never make a real Communist of an Irishman; their hereditary tradition, their racial characteristics—everything—is totally opposed to such a doctrine. Above all their faith is against such teaching. And that Faith you will never kill. Oh—I know there are bad Catholics—the drunkard, the wastrel, the utterly bad, but even though they lead bad lives—may even leave the Faith altogether for a while—still they believe. Oh—I could tell you tales! But no matter—you will see for yourself before long. And now, tell me something about yourself—will you? You remind me of one whom I knew long ago.'

'There is not much to tell. My father is dead—both he and mother were Irish—and I was born in London—in Whitechapel. My sister is married there, and now I have got work here, and my mother is with me.'

He spoke in short sentences, as if the subject of his family were a distasteful one—as indeed it was. His Cockney accent struck unpleasantly upon the ears that were used to the kindly Irish tongue. He would speak no more about himself, so that Nora remained in ignorance of his identity.

He asked presently about the state of the country, about which, however, he showed little interest. He found both Nora and Rose inclined to be reticent—Nora especially so. As for them, they were perfectly amazed that anyone living in Dublin during those fateful days of May, 1922, could be absolutely ignorant of the powder-mine which might explode at any moment. However, it was not their business to enlighten him, and anyhow Rose knew little that was definite, and Nora would not have dreamt of confiding in a stranger.

Presently he got up to say 'Goodnight,' telling them that he was grateful for their kindness, and that his mother would be expecting him.

'You must bring your mother to see us—come in any evening, you will always be welcome,' said Nora.

He coloured shyly.

'My mother never visits anywhere,' he said, 'Goodnight—and thank you again.'

'What a queer individual!' exclaimed Nora.

'A little bit off the thatch, if you ask me!' replied Rose. 'He and his Communism! Is the man a fool that he cannot see that the people have something else to think about just now than this foreign trash! Well—I'm off to bed—goodnight, old girl!'

'Goodnight, my dear—sleep well!'

But Nora herself did not sleep well. Who was this young man with the face of Victor Hewdon, with certain of his mannerisms, who yet spoke with the accents of Whitechapel, and was shy and gauche, evidently conscious of these defects in himself? A strange combination, and a disquieting one to Nora Harding.

That night for the first time, for many a year, she was back again in Larramore, standing in the porch of her cottage, listening for the sound of Victor's footsteps coming along the country road. And when she awoke her pillow was wet with tears.

After that first night, George found himself often dropping into the flat below his own. He liked a cup of coffee and a talk; if there was another attraction, he did not admit it even to himself.

Sometimes other people were there; people with whom he felt ill at ease, a fish out of water; people who chattered in French to Rose, and who seemed to think that Literature, Art, the Theatre, were the most important things in the world. He hated them, yet envied them, was jealous of them against his will and what he considered to be his better judgment. He wished his mother would accompany him sometimes, for he guessed instinctively that she would be able to talk their language, think their thoughts, albeit she had been a stranger to all that for so many years.

Others, too, came to the flat. Young men, well drilled, keen, alert, who eyed his sallow face and stooped shoulders with what he took to be contempt. Queer fellows, he thought them; young men who could be serious enough, often looking grim and determined, and yet could laugh and jest at anything and everything. His Whitechapel outlook and mentality could not understand them.

When June came, he noticed that Nora Harding—with whom he had grown very friendly—was looking worried, anxious. He noticed, too, the air of unrest, of tension; the very streets seemed to breathe it. As for his organising work, it was useless going among the people, they simply would not be bothered with him. In vain he preached his Brotherhood of Man, his International aims, the abolition of Capitalists. At best they regarded him as a crank, or harmless lunatic; others, not so tolerant, glanced at him askance, thinking him an emissary from the enemies of the Catholic Church. At the time Communism was little known or talked about in Ireland, besides which, the minds of the people were occupied with the division in their own ranks, with the terrible spectre of civil war looming on the horizon. George Dempsey and his theories were of no account with the Dublin folk in the month of June, 1922.

One morning he accompanied his mother to Mass to the Jesuit Church, where she went each morning at seven o'clock. He had not been many days in Dublin before noticing the strong hold which their Faith had upon the people. He went to this early Mass to see for himself how they attended. He was astounded at the large congregation, at the number of Communicants thronging the altar rails. Old and young, rich and poor, were there. Workmen on their way to their day's toil; office girls, clerks, teachers, factory workers, poor women from the neighbouring slums, school children, Old Age Pensioners. One and all alike, in that they worshipped at the same altar, were faithful to the same creed.

Coming back from the church, walking that short distance at the side of his mother, George felt depressed, unhappy. For the first time he fully realised the mighty forces which were arrayed against him. Communism and the Catholic Church were poles apart, and there seemed little doubt as to which was the stronger power in Ireland. Poor deluded creatures, he thought, doped by their priests. Would they ever cast off the shackles of superstition for the light of reason?

To his mother he said little, while she, delighted that he had gone with her to Mass, redoubled her prayers for his spiritual salvation.

CHAPTER XI

'DORAN'S'

'Put a bandage on this, will you, nurse? It's not much.'

Nurse Harding glanced at the boy's arm.

'It's nasty enough, Paddy,' she said. 'Won't you wait and have a stitch put in?'

'No—I haven't time—it will be all right.'

'How are you getting on out there?'

'Not too bad, but the enemy are giving it to us pretty hot. I say, nurse, we would give the world for a cup of tea! The firing makes you that parched! It's awful!'

'I'll get it for you. How many of you are there?'

'Ten.'

'Right! I'll be out in a few moments with a tray to gladden your hearts.'

'The adjutant will kill you, nurse!'

'Will he, indeed? Let him try!'

She turned to Rose O'Daly, who had been watching her.

'Help me to get a big pot of tea—cut some bread—those poor boys have been under fire for hours.'

It was soon ready, and the two women carried it out through the back yard of the hotel, and then standing at a certain distance called to the men. One came running to fetch the tea, and the rest raised a cheer. Fortunately the adjutant was not in sight!

It was Thursday, 29th June, 1922. Dublin was in the grip of civil war; all who possibly could do so kept within doors, no sounds were to be heard by day or night save the rattle of machine guns, the deadly crack, crack, from the rifle of the sniper on some roof, the boom, boom, of the guns from the Four Courts.

The IRA were in possession of Doran's Hotel, and Nora Harding was in charge of the Red Cross there. Two other nurses were with her, two doctors, and several members of the Cumman na mBan, who did the cooking and helped in every way. The women kept mostly to the basement, where one room was turned into a hospital of sorts, and where, too, was the big kitchen where the men came for their meals. The cellar of the hotel was also in the basement, and this was guarded by an elderly man—past fighting age although he would not admit the fact—who saw to it that no one entered except the medical staff or the commandant. Not that the men tried to enter, they were as sober a crowd as one could find.

The street where 'Doran's' was situated was full of other hotels, large and small. The garrison in Doran's Hotel numbered from 150 to 200. Some of these men were billeted in other hotels, breaches in the wall having been made for purposes of communication. In the street without, mines had been laid, and now and then there would be a shout from the window—'mind the mine!' as some poor neutral person tried to get through the street.

On that morning, the feast day of SS Peter and Paul, Nora had gone to Mass in the Pro-Cathedral close by. Rose had been with her, and another of the nurses. How strange the streets seemed! Deadly quiet in the summer dawn, just a few women slipping out to Mass, glancing nervously around them as they sped quickly on their way. One of these, old, bent, but with bright eager eyes had stopped Nora.

'Are you from Doran's?'

'Yes.'

'Thank God! Will you tell me how my Paddy is? Doyle is his name—a young fella of eighteen. Do you know him?'

'I do,' replied Nora, with a smile, 'he is quite well and a fine soldier.'

'Not hurt, nurse darlint? Not wounded?'

'Not a scratch!'

'Thanks be! Well, let you tell him that his grannie says he is to keep on fightin', and never give in! Tell him if he's kilt itself it will be for Ireland, as his grandfather was on the hills beyant Tallaght when the Fenians were out in '67.'

She blessed the little group with the blessing of an old Irishwoman, and they felt the better for it.

Inside the cathedral all was quiet and strange. Even the Mass itself seemed hushed, as if over the very altar brooded the weight of a terrible wrong, brother rising against brother, father against son.

That afternoon, Nora was pouring out tea at the kitchen table, when a bullet crashed through the window, shattering the teapot in her hand as it passed by, and was embedded in the wall behind. She had not time to feel frightened, so quickly had it happened, hardly indeed did she realise her narrow escape. It was not until word came from the CO that all women were to leave the kitchen while the men put sandbags to the windows, that she knew she had been in danger.

They all gathered in the 'hospital' while this was being done—Nora, the two other nurses, the Cumann na mBan girls—those great souls who worked so hard, putting their hand to everything, never seeming tired or weary, always cheery and willing. Rose O'Daly had come to give a hand while she got copy for her French paper, and anyway, this sort of adventure was just what she loved. Nora was the real nurse; in her eyes a patient was a patient, be he one of their own 'boys', or one of the enemy. Not so, May Brennan, one of the other nurses; she could hardly bring herself to dress the wounds of the two prisoners who were in 'Doran's', and only her rigid hospital training and the example of Nora made her do so.

To this group now entered the MO, Dr Robert Givor—commonly known as 'Bobby Givor'. With him was Tom Miley, a Trinity student belonging to one of the most ultra Unionist families in Dublin. He was a hot Republican, and had joined up as a voluntary worker. He was not a soldier, but gave a hand at everything, being particularly useful in going for messages, getting through where the other men could not.

'What do you think happened Miley today?' asked Dr Givor. The MO was a big man, extremely tall, fair-haired, fresh complexioned, and as cheery a soul as one could meet. His great laugh could be heard all over 'Doran's'. Tom Miley, a slight, dark young man, rather precise and quiet, had 'Trinity' written all over him.

'What was it?' asked Nora.

Tom Miley smiled.

'I was sent across the city,' he said, 'and when passing Leinster House I saw some fellows in the window. I took them to be ours, and called out "Hello!" They called back and asked how we were getting on. I said all was fine. "Where are you?" they asked then. "Doran's," I replied. And you should have seen the change that came over the scene. One glance at their faces was enough. I did not stay on—but went!'

Nora laughed.

'You *would* get into some mistake like that!' she said.

'By the way, nurse,' interposed Dr Givor, 'they have sent over from Garry's to know if I can spare Dr Donnelly? Can we get on without him, do you think?'

'Of course—with you in residence! Anyway we will have to manage if they want him in Garry's, for I know they have a lot of casualties there.'

'Any tea going?' asked the doctor. It was his one panacea for all evils—a cup of strong tea.

'In a few moments—we are temporarily evicted from the kitchen,' replied Nora, and she told him the tale of 'The Bullet and the Teapot,' as it was afterwards called in the annals of 'Doran's'.

He looked grave for once.

'You had a narrow escape,' he said, 'and we could not afford to lose you.'

'Well, come along, and I'll give you tea now—for I hear them leaving the kitchen.'

And just then two of the men came to report that the nurses could now return to the kitchen where the sandbags were in position.

The larder at 'Doran's' was kept well supplied by the foraging parties who went out each day to bring in what was wanted. Nothing easier than this! Cans of milk were taken from the milk carts, loaves from the bakers. Nora would never forget the first morning she saw the milkman bringing in two of his huge cans, and the man off the baker's cart following with a stack of loaves. Meat came the same way, and all else they wanted. The shopkeepers gave willingly enough for the most part, the unwilling ones found themselves looking at a revolver.

Rose O'Daly was delighted with all this, and even persuaded two of the men to take her out with them one day. The CO hearing of it, she was reprimanded and also the men. Nora was very angry about the matter, and Rose, really penitent for once, never asked to go again.

'Captain O'Grady says will you go upstairs, please nurse—he wants you.'

Nora went with the man who had brought the message, and in the hall she found Captain O'Grady and a few other men. Leaning against the big marble topped table, she saw a boy of about fifteen, crying in a forlorn fashion; his sobs were jerky, nervous, and his hands clung to the table as if he feared being taken away.

'What is the matter with him?' she asked.

The captain saluted smartly.

'My men brought him in from the street,' he said, 'the little chap seems to have lost his head entirely—he thinks we are going to shoot him! We have talked in vain to him, so I thought it best to send for you, nurse.'

Nora sat down on a couch, and made the boy sit beside her. He was trembling all over, and held on to her hands as if he would never let them go.

'Don't let them shoot me! Please don't let them shoot me!' he kept saying.

'But they would not touch you,' cried Nora, 'they only want to be friends with you. Come, tell me what happened and how you were out by yourself in the streets?'

Bit by bit, she learned that his aunt, with whom he lived, had sent him out to look for bread, thinking he would get through the streets safer than an adult. He had grown nervous on finding himself practically alone, the sound of the constant firing frightened him, and then as he was nearing Doran's Hotel, there was a shout of 'mind the mine!' and losing his head entirely, he had fled, panic-stricken, right into the danger zone. One of the men had reached him in time, and carried him, struggling frantically, into the hotel. They had tried to laugh him out of his fears, but he could not believe they were not going to shoot him, so they had sent for Nora, rightly thinking that this was a case for her. It took her some little time to allay the boy's fears, but she succeeded at last. He was taken downstairs and given some hot milk by Rose who joked and laughed with him, until he smiled at her, almost in spite of himself. They gave him a couple of loaves and sent him home under escort of two cheery Boy Scouts.

The next morning, from the street without, could be heard the cry 'Stop Press! Republic Stop Press!' and presently Dr Givor came in with a copy of the daily slip, bright pink in colour, which carried the news of the day to the various garrisons.

'War News. No. 4. Friday, June 30th, 1922. Seventh Year of the Republic.'

Hastily she threw her eyes over the contents.

'The Fight goes on! The Four Courts have been bombarded, smashed to pieces, burnt out, gutted by Macready's 60 pounder guns and mines. There was nothing left for the gallant garrison to hold. All honour to them for having held it so long in a hell of fire.

Then came the Capture of Transport. Firing on Red Cross. British Co-operation. Not much news in reality; just a try at making the best of things; a gallant effort to keep up the hearts of those who were fighting so hard.

That evening a young Franciscan priest came to Doran's to hear Confessions, and prepare the garrison to meet death, should it come, like good Christians and gallant Irishmen. He was young and fair-haired, with an almost ethereal look of delicacy, and had walked the streets alone, perhaps the only one who could have done so in safety that Friday night when things were drawing towards an end as far as 'Doran's' was concerned.

Nora and the other women went to Confession also. The men were lined up in a long queue outside the room where the Franciscan sat. A sombre silence held them all; they realised that for some of them this would be the last Confession. Quietly, with reverent concentration, they stood there awaiting their turn, while their rosaries slipped through their fingers. When they saw the girls, they gave place to them at once.

Two of the garrison were badly wounded that night. Dr Givor and the nurses worked heroically in the tiny 'hospital' in the basement, but the cases were hospital ones, and the ambulance men—to whom be all honour for the manner in which they answered calls during that terrible time—came and took them to hospital.

None of the garrison thought of sleep that night, indeed all through the week they had had but little. Nora had seen men staggering on their feet, with glazed eyes, literally stupid for want of it, and on several occasions she had simply insisted that they should lie down for a few hours. She herself, looking back afterwards upon that week, could not remember one sound sleep which she had had. The firing was so near, so incessant that if one did lie down the shots seemed to be in the very room.

It was about midnight and Nora and Rose happened to be in the hall talking to the CO, when the guard on the door opened it in response to a summons from without. Three of the men entered, accompanied by a prisoner.

Rose gave a sudden cry, and Nora, glancing at the man, saw that it was George Dempsey.

'Do you know him?' asked the Commandant.

'Yes—he lives in the same house, he has the flat above us.'

'Tell us what you know about him,' at the same time motioning to the men to remove George out of earshot.

'Well, I think he is harmless,' replied Nora, 'he comes from London, and his English accent may have roused the men's suspicions.'

She then told him all she knew about George Dempsey.

'A Communist—eh?' said the CO. 'I wonder? I bet you any money you like the fellow is just a spy!'

'Oh no, I am sure he is not! He knows nothing about Ireland really, and is full of those ridiculous ideas of the universal Brotherhood of Man and so forth—please do not hurt him!'

It was Rose O'Daly who spoke, and the Commandant glanced curiously at her. It was a time when one came to suspect people for very little.

'No harm will be done to him for the present,' He replied curtly. 'If we find evidence that he is really a spy—well, that will be another matter.'

He turned away as he spoke, and went to interview the prisoner. Nora, knowing better than to say any more, was turning away when again the door was unbarred and two men entered, half-leading, half-carrying, a young fellow of about twenty. He was bleeding profusely from a wound in the arm, and weak from the loss of blood. The nurses got him downstairs at once, and as it was but a flesh wound, though deep enough, the arm was cleaned and dressed, and the usual treatment given.

He fell asleep presently from the effects of the opiate, and Nora stood beside the bed looking at him. Dark and good looking, he was now pale, haggard, worn, with deep circles beneath the eyes as if he had not slept for many hours.

It was late morning before he awoke, starting up in sudden fear as if he had fallen asleep while on duty. The men had told Nora that he had been sent from Garry's Hotel to carry a despatch to the CO at Doran's, and had been wounded by a sniper on the way. He had just managed to stagger on, and when he came in sight of Doran's the men had brought him in.

'Where am I?' he asked.

'In Doran's Hotel. You were brought in wounded last night. You are all right.'

'And the despatch?'

'The Commandant has it safe.'

'Oh—I am so glad.'

'What is your name?' asked Nora.

This boy with the cultured accent, the gentle manner, was a stranger to her, although she knew many of those now stationed at Garry's Hotel.

He raised his dark eyes and smiled at her.

'Hugh Hewdon,' he replied.

CHAPTER XII

THE SUNDAY

On the Sunday of that fateful week, machine-gun fire was opened on Doran's Hotel from the direction of Amiens Street, and from the bottom of Gardiner Street, near Beresford Place.

The Commandant sent for Nora Harding.

'The enemy are opening heavy fire upon us,' he said, 'we cannot expect to hold Doran's much longer. We are going to evacuate and try to reach the Gresham. We will go through the Continental Hotel—we can get that way through the breaches in the walls—and are taking with us the wires attached to the mines. We will explode the mine from there, and wreck this building. I should advise all the women to leave now.'

'Not those of the Red Cross,' replied Nora quietly, 'we must be the last to leave the building. It is our duty to remain until the last of the garrison have gone.'

'Very well—as you wish.'

The Commandant was worried, anxious; he was young, and felt his responsibility acutely, being desirous that the loss of life in his garrison at 'Doran's' should be as small as possible.

Swiftly, quietly, the men got away, and when the last one was gone, the little band of Red Cross workers took refuge in the cellar of the 'Continental' some three doors away. Through the breaches in the walls they crept, and made their way down to the damp, mouldy cellar. There were twelve of them: Nora, Rose, the two other nurses, four Cumann na mBan girls, Dr Givor, Tom Miley, and the wounded boy, Hugh Hewdon. They also had with them, the prisoner, George Dempsey. He had been given to Nora, who had vouched for his behaviour, and as he seemed so harmless, she was to let him return to the flat when she reached it herself. That is if she ever did reach it.

The little company carried bundles containing all their belongings—nightdress, comb, change of underclothes, etc., besides which they had surgical dressings, the Red Cross flag, and other items. They put Nora in mind of the poor Belgian refugees who used to come to Dublin during the European war, and whom she had often nursed.

There, in the cellar, the Rosary was started, all joining, except Tom Miley, Hugh Hewdon, and George Dempsey. They stood against the wall, watching the others on their knees, and then presently Hugh knelt down beside Nora and said his own prayers. Miley followed his example; only George remained standing, sullen, remote, half bewildered by this strange atmosphere into which he had suddenly found himself precipitated.

And so they waited for what might well be the end—for all present knew that when the mine exploded it might be their last moment on earth. Nora tried to pray, to make her peace with God, to be ready to meet Him; it was all in vain, she could not concentrate on anything except the question of the mine. She could feel her heart beating against her side, thumping, thumping. How much longer would it beat? Would the mine never go off? What were the men doing not to let it off before this. Far better that the end should come quickly than this fearful suspense.

The Rosary was finished. Silence followed, save for a muffled prayer from the women, a cough from the doctor, the restless walking up and down of Tom Miley. Nora, her face in her hands, felt a movement beside her, a hand seeking hers. Hugh Hewdon still sick, weak from the loss of blood, had crept close to her. She put her arms around him holding him tightly, speaking comforting words to him, just as a mother might have done. She might have been his mother as far as age went; she might have been it in reality, had things happened differently many years ago. So she soothed him, holding his hand, and he was glad to be near her, thinking she was like his mother. Manly and brave though the lad was, he had gone through much; sick and giddy, he had been obliged to leave the comparative safety of the 'hospital' in 'Doran's' and join the fugitives in the cellar, where the long wait was getting badly on his nerves.

At last! A roar, devastating, terrific, shook the cellar so that the very walls seemed to quake. It died away, was followed by a pause, and each one sat up, looking at one another, wondering if it was really over—the fearful ordeal of suspense which seemed unending.

'Are we really alive—or are we not?' asked Rose.

'Alive and kicking!' replied Tom Miley breathing a great sigh of relief. 'Good heavens! That was the longest half hour I ever went through!'

'Half hour?' repeated Rose. 'Do you mean that that YEAR we have just spent was only half an hour!'

Shaky, giddy, feeling as if the world was still rocking around them, the little band staggered through the breach in the wall and made their way into the apparently deserted street. They carried the Red Cross flag, the nurses were in uniform, yet fire was open upon them as they went along. Fortunately no one was hit, and they reached Marlborough Street, and heard a welcome shout from a public-house near one of the corners. There they found the garrison from Doran's Hotel, who had been compelled to take refuge there on their way to the Gresham.

In after years, the events of that evening were more or less blurred in Nora's memory. She remembered sitting on the floor in one of the rooms in that public-house; she sat between two windows from both of which the men were replying to the fire of the enemy, as fast as they could; she was consumed with a terrific thirst, and some one gave her a bottle of lemonade, and one of soda water; these she held in either hand, drinking first from one, then from the other, oblivious of everything but her fearful thirst. After that they had found themselves in the room of a tenement house close by, and there the woman made them tea. Nora often afterwards looked for that house, but she could never identify it, and as she never heard the name of the woman, she was not able to find her. That cup of tea—the kind she would not have touched at home, being strong and sweet—was the most delightful she had ever drunk.

And then, later on in the evening, they at length reached the Gresham, the Headquarters of the IRA at that time.

Here all was bustle and movement, officers coming and going, men with despatches, who had managed to make their way through the streets; intelligence officers with the latest news. The garrison from Doran's Hotel were lined up and inspected by one of the Chief of Staff. Nora caught a glimpse of the 'Chief' himself— Eamon de Valera; she saw too, for a passing moment, Cathal Brugha, as he went by with some other officers. Little did she think that she was never to see him alive again.

She and the others were presently handed over to the members of the Cumann na mBan and the other voluntary workers, and were given a good supper. Nora ate and drank as one in a dream—she was too tired to even take an interest in what was going on. Yet the great table was crowded with men and women, all from different places, all with stories to tell. Tongues wagged freely, and Rose was in her element, laughing, talking, apparently not tired at all. George Dempsey hardly spoke, he was furious to think that he had got mixed up with these foolish people, playing their silly game of war, pretending to be patriots, plunging their country into chaos, putting back the clock of Progress. In his eyes they were fools, and worse than fools. And here he was in their midst arrested on the chance that he might be a spy! He was worried too about his mother—she would be terribly anxious about him. He could hardly reply civilly when spoken to, and was gruff even when Rose spoke to him, turning away from her laughing glance in sullen silence.

The meal over, Nora and Rose with the two other nurses were shown a large bedroom which they were to share between them. The Cumann na mBan girl who showed them the room, told them that she would not wake them till late in the morning.

'You must be frightfully tired—indeed you look it—after all you have gone through. So sleep well now—Goodnight!'

It seemed too good to be true that they could really go to bed and sleep—not merely lie down for a couple of hours in their clothes. All that week they had never undressed when lying down to sleep, only to wash themselves; now they really undressed, got into their nighties, and climbed into the big comfortable beds. Nora, with a great sigh of relief, put out her hand to switch off the light beside her bed.

And even as she did so, while her hand was still stretched out, quick running steps came down the corridor, stopped at the door, upon which sounded a great knocking, while a voice called:

'You are to get up at once and report downstairs in the "hospital". The enemy are opening machine-gun fire on us in five minutes.'

Stupidly, like one dazed, Nora stumbled from bed.

'Well—I should certainly call this a day!' remarked one of the nurses, who was lately back from New York.

'I should call it Life—with a big L!' said Rose O'Daly. In a few moments they were all downstairs once more, in the big room which had been fitted up as a 'hospital'. It was crowded with the Red Cross Staffs from other parts who had made their way to the Gresham; medical men and nurses were there; voluntary workers and also about a dozen prisoners. It was but a short time before they received the order for all women and prisoners to leave the building at once. Nora thought it must have been about two o'clock in the morning when the order came to them.

It came as a thunderclap—hardly could they believe their ears. Never, for one moment, had they anticipated this. They might be shot dead, the building might be set on fire, but that they should be ordered to leave it—to go away just because they were women, to be sent out of the hotel, not be allowed to stay and see the finish—it was beyond belief. They even dared to protest, to detain the harassed adjutant who had come with the order. It was useless. They were to leave—and immediately.

Feeling humiliated, crushed, disappointed, they put on their coats, and following two officers through long corridors, by underground passages, eventually emerged into the streets. Dark, deserted, empty, seemed those streets, yet hidden Death lurked at every corner, from every roof, dogged their steps as they sped along, going their various ways. Some took refuge in the houses of friends, others spent part of the night in the old Protestant Church of St Thomas, others who, like Nora, lived near, managed to make their way home.

It was a nightmare journey through a city of the Inferno. Although the distance from the Gresham to George Square was very short, it seemed to be miles that night. There was a sniper on a roof somewhere near, they could not locate his position, which made matters worse, and the sound of his revolver going off—crack, crack—every few minutes, got on Nora's nerves. Reaching the Square, they seemed to be alone in the world—just the four of them—Rose, Nora, George Dempsey, and young Hewdon. Nora had brought him with her—she felt that she must save his life if possible.

The house at last. George, who had not spoken since they left the Gresham, took out his latch key and opened the door, and they passed into the comparative safety of the flat. Then without a word, a look in their direction, he went straight upstairs to his mother, and Nora and Rose helped Hugh to their flat, and got him to bed in Nora's room, while she shared Rose's. He was soon asleep, and the two friends after a bath and hot tea felt different beings. Sleep seemed to have fled, so excited, so keyed up were they both, yet when they went to bed they slept soundly, undisturbed by the constant firing to which they were now so accustomed.

At noon, Nora awoke to the sound of a knock on the door. Hastily flinging on her dressing-gown she opened it to find Mrs Dempsey standing on the threshold. She was surprised, and still half asleep, remained staring at the woman, stupidly. Then:

'Please come in,' she said.

Mrs Dempsey had never entered the flat before; she always refused when Nora asked her—through George—to come and take a cup of tea and have a chat. Why had she come now? Perhaps George—

'Your son? Is he ill? Perhaps he was not able for what we had to go through—he does not look strong.'

'George is all right—he is sleeping. But Hugh—Hugh Hewdon—how is he? He is wounded, I think?'

Nora had brought her into the sitting-room of the flat. The summer sun was shining on the dust of a week, on dead flowers which had been fresh when she had hurriedly left for Doran's Hotel. Was it a week ago—or a year? She glanced curiously at the woman before her, and again that haunting sense of familiarity—of having met her somewhere—of having spoken to her in the past—came to Nora. Yet she did not know this woman, middle-aged, gaunt, with lines of trouble deeply marked upon her tired face. Surely she was a stranger to her. And yet—

'Hugh Hewdon? Do you know him, then?'

'Yes—he is my nephew.'

Enlightenment came then, swift, certain.

'Your nephew? You—you are Anne Hewdon!'

'I was Anne Hewdon—I am now Anne Dempsey. You don't remember me, I suppose. You are Miss Harding. I recognised you the first moment we met—that evening in the hall.'

'Of course I remember you! I am so glad to meet you again. I will just see how Hugh is, and if he is awake you can see him.'

Anne detained her as she was leaving the room.

'It is probable that the boy has never heard of me,' she said, 'so do not say that his aunt wants to see him—I will just be a friend of yours. That will be best for the present.'

Hugh was awake and feeling better, so Anne Dempsey, in the character of the 'lady from the flat above', went in to see him. Her eyes filled with involuntary tears as she looked at this boy—her brother's son—heir to Ballafagh, who, in all probability, would some day be Master in her old home. He did not resemble her brother, but he was like the Larramore family, having the same clear cut features, brilliant eyes, and rather impulsive manner. A handsome boy of about twenty years—a man, no doubt, in his own opinion. He spoke with the familiar accents of her girlhood, his voice was that of an Irish gentleman—than which there is no better to be heard.

And her own son? The contrast moved her painfully. George spoke in the accents of Whitechapel; his whole outlook on life was coloured by his upbringing in London's East End; he lived and moved and had his being in its very roots. And yet he too, was a Hewdon. Oh! her criminal folly! How dearly she had paid—and was still paying—for it.

Anne was as conservative in her opinions as on the day she left Ballafagh. Far more so, indeed, for on that day she had thrown convention and tradition to the four winds of heaven, and set off on the path of adventure. The adventure had turned out a sordid one, repentance had come quickly in its wake, and Anne, regretting every day of her life the one false step which she had taken, wept in ashes and sackcloth because she had ever gone against the traditions of her class, against every ideal and tenet which she had been taught.

For his part, Hugh saw only a rather quiet woman, not good-looking, quite old in his eyes and not particularly interesting. He was tired, his wound was painful, and he did not talk much to her then. However, during the next few days, as he became more himself, and his wound began to heal, he took an interest again in life, and Nora and Rose found him a delightful companion. He was boyish for his age, and yet wise in many ways. He told them all about his home at Ballafagh, of his mother, who had taught him to be an Irishman—'really Irish, like Tone and Emmet, you know, Miss Harding'—of the gardens, his pony, the people he knew in Larramore. Of his father he spoke with some reserve.

When Nora questioned him about his grandmother, he said that she had died two years ago. Then, with sudden surprise in his voice, he said: 'But how did you know I had a grandmother? I do not think I mentioned her—did I?'

Nora was silent for a moment. Then she said: 'Would it surprise you very much to know that I once lived at Larramore? I was the District Nurse there a long time ago—before you were born. I knew your grandmother well, but never met your mother.'

'My mother is lovely—everyone says she is the most beautiful woman in the country. You know my grandfather was Lord Larramore—and she was the loveliest of the family.'

'I remember your Uncle Dermot. I suppose he has the title now?'

'Oh yes—but he is no good! Just a regular Britisher.'

Nora laughed.

'But most of your family were. Mrs Hewdon must be an exception.'

'There were others too—all down the years. Mother has told me about them.'

'How did you happen to be in the fighting here? Were you in Dublin?'

'Yes—I'm in Trinity. I know Mr Miley there—but he is older than I am, so I don't see much of him. Still I knew he was one of us. There were more too—they are all out.'

'Have you written home?'

'Yes—just a few lines. I told mother I was all right. I could say no more, of course. She will think I am in college, because I put no address on the letter. I wonder if father took any part in things this time? He is getting old, you know'—Nora smiled to herself a trifle sadly—'so perhaps he stayed at home. But he is very bitter—a strict old Die Hard!'

'Yes—so I can imagine.'

'Why—did you know my father also?'

'Yes.'

There was a pause, which Hugh broke by saying: 'That lady upstairs—Mrs Dempsey—she puzzles me tremendously. You know the son is an awful bounder, and then he is a Communist or something of the sort. But she herself—she seems like one of ourselves. I feel quite at home with her. But the son—he is impossible! Why—he hasn't an Aitch to his name!'

Nora looked curiously at the boy; he was so young, so brave, willing to risk his life at any moment; yet imbued too, with all the prejudices of his class, all the arrogance of youth. She had grown fond of him, both for his own sake, and because he was his father's son, but she was doubtful as to how he would react to the shock of learning who Mrs Dempsey really was. Still he must be told, and as well now as later. Besides, they did no know what any day might bring forth now.

'Did you ever hear your mother speak of a sister of your father? Anne was her name.'

The boy flushed

'I heard my grandmother say something about her to mother one day. I could not help hearing. Afterwards I asked mother, and she told me that dad had a sister who ran away with someone very much beneath her. She said she was never spoken about in the family, and mother did not know where she was.'

'Would it surprise you very much to hear that Mrs Dempsey is your Aunt Anne? She married Patrick Dempsey, who was gardener's boy in Ballafagh House when I was District Nurse in Larramore, and they ran away. I never heard what became of her until I met her the other day, and she told me who she was.'

Hugh was staring at her with pale face, and wide open eyes. Hardly could he credit what she was telling him. Poor Aunt Anne, she must have had a time! No wonder she looked so worn and haggard. Then a sudden thought came to him.

'Then her son—that awful bounder——'

'The "awful bounder" is your first cousin,' said Nora.

To herself she added; 'And the next heir to Ballafagh, if anything should happen to this boy.'

CHAPTER XIII

WHAT HAPPENED AT MARGALLIN

'Hands up! Put them up! Line up on the bridge there, and be quick about it!'

Nora Harding, standing thus on the bridge hands stretched above her head, arms growing tired, gazed into the face of the man who stood in front of her, revolver in hand. He did not seem too sure as to how it should be held, the hand holding it being decidedly shaky. She wished he did not look so nervous.

Facing each prisoner, there stood a man with a revolver; some of them in uniform of sorts, others in any kind of garments. There was a sergeant in charge, and he had sent a man to the barracks in the town of Margallin, a quarter of a mile beyond the bridge, to inform the CO that there had been a capture of a lorry full of 'Irregulars'. While waiting for an officer to arrive, he saw to it that the prisoners were closely guarded. Those prisoners were four women, Dr Givor, Tom Miley, the man who had driven the car, and Hugh Hewdon.

Nora took a deep breath of weariness. Would they never let her put her hands down again? On her left—she could just see her out of the corner of her eye—was Rose O'Daly, and next to her again, May Cross, one of the nurses who had been sent with this expedition which was trying to get Red Cross supplies to the western districts where the men were badly in need of them. There was another nurse too, Bride Clooney, but Nora could not see her from where she stood. Dr Givor and Tom Miley were further down on her right, but when she dared to turn her head, ever so slightly, to try and locate them, a sharp command from the shaky individual, who held the revolver, made her stand rigid again. It was Hugh whom she wanted to see most; Hugh, who should not be there at all. He had been left in the flat under care of Mrs Dempsey, but had managed to get out without her knowledge, and turned up at the house in Eccles Street, from where the little party were to start on the western adventure. Seeing him standing there, talking to other young fellows in the doorway, his arm still in a sling, Nora had implored him to go back. He had refused, and when they got into their transport conveyance, insisted on getting in with them. Their car was a van belonging to Taylor's, of Grafton Street, and by no means an ideal carriage. The name had been painted out, and the van otherwise camouflaged.

The first part of the journey was rather amusing than dangerous—one never knew who or what would appear on the road to challenge them. However, with only a few small adventures, they reached Margallin Bridge, a short distance outside the town itself. Margallin was a fair sized town in the midlands, and they had expected there might be some difficulty in getting through. Still they had experienced a definite feeling of surprise when the command to halt, followed by the call 'put them up!' had fallen upon their ears. They had the Red Cross flag on the lorry, but their assertion that they only carried Red Cross supplies was laughed at. They were spies, they were told. Word had come that they were leaving Dublin, and would be at Margallin about midnight, and now they were under arrest, lined up on the bridge, where they had to stay until the CO from the barracks came to inspect them, and say what was to be done. So much the sergeant had told them.

'Surely you will allow the ladies to put down their hands now?' presently asked Dr Givor.

'How do we know that they are ladies? More likely to be men dressed up—we know your sort!'

Although summer, the night was cold. Nora also suffered from the cold of nervousness—or rather nervous tension. She was no coward, but the uncertainty, the shaky hands of the man holding the revolver, the cramp in her strained arms—all combined to make her feel decidedly shivery. At the moment a clock in the near distance boomed out twelve sonorous strokes, and a soft voice murmured: 'I stood on the bridge at midnight, when the clocks were striking the hour——'

It was Rose Daly, standing a few paces away.

'She will see the funny side of Death—crack a joke with him when he comes for her,' thought Nora. A sharp reprimand—'No whispering there!' brought silence once more.

How long—how very long—it seemed before the CO from the barracks in Margallin arrived to take charge. He came on a motor cycle, two other men with him. An aggressive, domineering bully, he treated them at once as prisoners—and dangerous ones. To all representations that they were Red Cross workers, and so protected under that flag, he turned a deaf ear, pooh-poohing the idea as absurd.

'You will hear more of this,' stormed Dr Givor. 'You are acting against all international laws of civilised warfare. You cannot arrest Red Cross workers!'

His words went unheeded. The women were put back into the van in charge of the sergeant, and with them went Hugh, to his own disgust; however, the CO, seeing he was wounded thought it would look well if he drove him in the van, in place of ordering him to walk behind with the other men and the escort.

Inside the van two long seats, like benches, ran along both sides; on one of these sat the sergeant and Hugh; opposite to them were the two nurses, Rose O'Daly and Nora. The space between was so narrow that their knees almost touched. The CO from Margallin drove the car himself, and drove swiftly, nearly recklessly, as if he were in a hurry to reach the town. In a few seconds the men of the party and their escort were left far behind, and the van and its occupants sped through the dark countryside. There was silence and darkness within the van, each full of their own thoughts. Nora wondered what the others were thinking about; for her part, she was making conjectures as to where they were going, and how they would be treated; she was fearfully anxious, too, about Hugh. The boy had endeared himself greatly to her while sharing her flat, and she hoped no danger would now befall him. She could not see him, she did not care to speak, but she sensed that he was sitting very upright opposite to her, as far away from the sergeant as he could get.

They must have been but a short distance outside the town of Margallin, when like a bomb-shell, the command 'Halt!' sounded from the road without. The driver of the van shouted something back; Nora could not hear what he said, and it had no effect, for as he continued to drive on, fire was at once opened upon the van. A deadly fire, bullets spattering around like a shower of hailstones. The van had been going so swiftly that the driver found it impossible to pull up when called upon to do so; he kept shouting to the attackers, and now Nora could distinguish some of the words: 'Stop—damn you—stop! I am the CO from the barracks—cease fire! Good God—will you stop!'

Inside the van there was silence; the silence of complete bewilderment, causing a paralysis of the faculties. They waited there, expecting every second that they would be hit, but the bullets passed over them in some miraculous manner, to be embedded in the opposite side of the van. Nora tried to make an Act of Contrition, but her mind seemed numb. Beside her, she could now hear Rose saying softly, over and over again: 'Mon dieu! Mon Dieu!' while from the two other girls little sighs and gasps could be heard from time to time.

Who were the attacking party? Was it an ambush? If so, was there any chance of rescue? If an ambush, those attacking could not know that there were women in the van. At last the van could be felt slowing down, and the man driving it was heard talking to the attackers, calling them every kind of fool and imbecile—swearing at them for being lunatics. Then it was not an ambush? But why on earth were these men firing upon their own party? Nora leant forward and touched the sergeant. He was sitting exactly opposite to her, and she had been surprised that he had neither moved nor spoken—not even now, when the van had at last come to a standstill.

'What is it?' she asked him. 'Are those your men who fired upon us?'

There was no reply. The silence, the black darkness of the van's interior, seemed to hold something sinister. Hugh Hewdon had been seated beside the sergeant, and Nora now slid her hand in his direction. Finding his coat sleeve, she shook it gently.

'Hugh! Hugh! Don't you hear me? Are you—hurt?'

Even as she asked the question her hand came in contact with some warm sticky substance. With a little cry, she turned to the others.

'He is wounded—we must get him out of this!'

They tried to open the van door, but it was securely fastened. With their fists they banged at the window in front, calling out that someone was shot. The driver who had been engaged in wordy warfare with the firing party, now entered the van with several other men, flashing their torches around.

On the opposite seat to where the women sat were the two men of the party. Of these, the sergeant's body was sagging forward, eyes wide open staring at nothing, hands hanging by his side. He was stone dead, literally riddled by bullets. Beside him, Hugh Hewdon, badly wounded, still breathed.

Dr Givor's examination was barely over—the rest of the party had come up to them by this—before the van reached the town, and stopped at the entrance of the chief hotel. Although it was now nearly half-past one o'clock, the place was ablaze with light, and crowded with police and military, while others were passing in and out, and all was noise and confusion. The body of the sergeant was carried to a room, and Hugh was laid on a couch in the lounge. Nora, Rose O'Daly, and the two nurses stood beside him, and presently a pleasant looking young fellow of about nineteen brought them chairs. So bitterly was Nora feeling at the moment against every single man who had anything to do with the 'Free Staters', that she could hardly bring herself to accept even a chair. But Rose, with a sigh of relief sat down, as did the others, and Nora, seeing that the boy was looking quite hurt at her hesitation, took the seat and tried to smile her thanks.

Just then, Dr Givor, Tom Miley, and the other men of their party went past under escort. They were evidently being taken as prisoners. Where were they going? And what would become of the women—and especially of Hugh? Even while Nora was thinking thus, a smart, military looking man of middle-age—one who had 'Army Surgeon' written all over him—approached the couch where Hugh lay, and proceeded to examine him.

He bowed courteously to the girls, and comprehending at once that Nora was the eldest and probably in charge, spoke to her.

'The medical man who was with you,' he said, 'has told me about this boy. You are a nurse, I think?'

'Yes.'

'My name is Meehan. I was a surgeon in the army during the war. I think if we turn him this way, it will be better.'

Nora found herself compelled to like the man. They had one thing in common, a great love for their profession, and to both of them a patient was just a patient, be he friend or foe.

With the deft hands of the born surgeon, Dr Meehan, gently but thoroughly made his examination. When he had finished, he said to Nora: 'He has been shot through the lung—an hour, perhaps less, to live. Are you a relation?'

She shook her head dumbly. Rose, kneeling by the couch began to sob.

'You will know his people? His parents?'

'His name is Hugh Hewdon. His people live at Larramore, in Co Mayo.'

'Hewdon! The Hewdons of Co Mayo!'

Dr Meehan's face expressed amazement, horror. Imperceptibly he turned his head in the direction of a group standing a little distance away. It was composed of the CO who had driven their van; some of the men who had been their guard on the bridge, others who were apparently the firing party who had attacked the van in mistake, and a slight, gentlemanly looking man, who, although not in uniform, was evidently a soldier, and from what Nora could hear, had been in charge of the firing. His back was towards her, and he was facing Captain Doyle the CO, who was abusing him in no measured terms, and in a manner and expressions redolent of the slums from which he had emerged, to be given temporary command during this time of strife and terror.

'Blast you for a fool! If it wasn't your mistake, then who the hell was it? Weren't you in charge of the men? Didn't you give the order to fire? Deny it if you can—you dashed fool!'

'I am not denying it, Captain Doyle. But in giving the order I was but obeying you. You distinctly told me to open fire on any suspicious lorry—not even to wait and question them first. How was I to know that the van was driven by you, and not by Irregulars?'

'Have you no eyes in your head?'

'The night was too dark, and you drove too fast. It was impossible to distinguish you.'

'What! You dare to talk about my driving! You want to excuse yourself—you blithering idiot! You will hear more of this—that I can tell you!'

He strode off, and the man to whom he had been speaking turned his head, and Nora saw his face. Older, worn, with all the light of Youth and laughter gone from it—it was still the face of Victor Hewdon. She stifled the cry in her throat.

'You know Major Hewdon?' asked Dr Meehan.

'Yes—at least we knew each other once. Many years ago.'

'And this boy?'

'Yes—Hugh is his son.'

'Another tragedy of this cursed civil war! Brother against brother—father against son. I know Major Hewdon well—was through the war with him—a gentleman and a soldier, if ever there was one. And that Doyle, now in temporary command here, was a private in his regiment—a bad lot too. He's getting his own back—as he would say—on the major now. But how are we going to tell him about the boy?'

After all they had not to tell Victor Hewdon in so many words, for at that moment he happened to see Nora. He knew her at once, for changed though she was with the passing of the years, she was less changed than he was himself.

'Nora—Miss Harding! Is it really you?'

He came forward, hand outstretched. Nora's first thought was to stand in front of Hugh to spare Victor the shock until he had been in some measure prepared for it. But Hugh had seen his father. The boy had been lying with closed eyes, in a semi-conscious state, but now the eyes were open, and he was partly conscious for the moment.

'Dad!' he called, in a clear but weak voice.

'Hugh—you here!'

Major Hewdon was beside his son, kneeling by the couch, holding his hand in his.

'My boy—you are wounded? Not much, I hope?'

Then as the greyness of approaching death spread itself over the boy's features, his father turned to Nora.

'He is wounded. Is it——'

She looked at Dr Meehan. She simply could not speak.

Victor followed her glance, and a look of relief passed over his face.

'You here, doctor—I'm glad. How is the boy? He is my son, you know.'

'I know.'

Dr Meehan took Major Hewdon by the arm, and drew him aside. He never knew how he told him, but it was done somehow, and the major was back at his son's side. Hugh was still conscious and greeted his father with a smile.

'You here, Dad. Fighting—for the British?'

Each word was painful, difficult. Victor nodded his head.

Nora, at the other side of the bed, said softly: 'Don't try to speak, Hugh. Just say a little prayer in your mind—the Our Father.'

To her, as a Catholic, it seemed so strange that no priest was there, no prayers for the dying going up to heaven for this boy's soul. He tried to press her hand, to smile at her, but presently drifted away into unconsciousness again.

The minutes went by slowly. Men were passing and repassing through the lounge; voices were being raised in argument, orders were barked forth, waiters were carrying trays to and fro. To Nora, the whole thing seemed a phantasy—or rather a nightmare. That she should be kneeling there by the dying boy, and on the other side of the couch, Victor, holding his son's hands, watching his face for every change, standing at the entrance of the Valley of Death, unable to go further with his loved one.

About half an hour went by, and then the boy stirred, opened his eyes and smiled at his father.

'Dad—tell my mother—that I fought—and died—for Ireland. She will be — glad.'

They were his last words.

CHAPTER XIV

ROSE SAYS 'NO'

Rose O'Daly was powdering her face in front of the mirror on her toilet table. It was the month of August, and already the events of June and early July were things of the past. Back again in the flat, Nora at her work once more, Rose writing and enjoying life seemingly as much as ever, the adventures through which they had gone were as dreams. They were still subjected to raids at times, but were so used to these, that they were hardly upset by them.

Sometimes Nora would visit again in her sleep the bridge outside Margallin, and the man with the shaky hand would stand in front of her brandishing his revolver; or she was in the lounge at the hotel, seeing the anguish on Victor's face as he knelt beside his dying son; hearing, when Death had claimed his own, the exceeding bitter cry: 'Hugh—my son!' It had vividly brought to her mind, the great Biblical cry echoing down the ages—'Absalom—my son—my son!'

It had been his order to fire that had caused the death of his only son, and innocent though he might be in every sense of the word, Victor Hewdon could never forget that fact.

He had told Nora that he would come to Dublin to see his sister, for, after Hugh's death, she had told him all about Anne. So far he had not come, but he had written. Anne was rather glad that he had not come; she shrank painfully from meeting her brother, or anyone from her old world. But that he would come some day—probably soon—she knew.

Tonight, Rose was expecting a friend from Paris—one Antoine Dumont. She had not seen him for over a year, and as he happened to be a most particular friend, she was at great pains to make herself look especially charming. Nora, entering at the moment, told her that she was a perfect picture, but Rose, for once, was not satisfied with herself.

'Oh—but I am dowdy—a fright!'

Nora laughed more heartily than she had done for some time. Dowdy! Rose, the little Parisian to her finger tips—she to say she was dowdy! Such a word could never by any flight of the imagination be applicable to her.

'You are simply charming!' Nora cried. 'What a lovely frock! Where did you get it?'

'Mother sent it to me—do you like it?'

'Very much. At what hour do you expect Antoine?'

'In about half an hour. Is it not delightful to think that I shall see him again at last? And do you really think I will do? I am not then a dowdy one?'

She pirouetted in front of the wardrobe mirror, turning herself this way and that, trying to see herself from every possible angle. Nora, watching, thought what a delightful picture she made.

At the same hour that evening, upstairs in the top flat, George Dempsey was also putting the finishing touches to his toilet. Not that he had much to do; he simply washed his face and hands, brushed his hair—being careful of the parting in it—polished his shoes, and asked his mother for a clean handkerchief. He was attired in a badly cut 'reach-me-down' suit of navy blue, which was already losing its colour.

His mother was sitting in a chair by the open window. It was a close evening, and having cleared up after the 'tea-dinner', which she had prepared for George, she was glad to sit where she could get a breath of air, wafted in from the old city square.

'Are you going out, George?' she asked.

'Not just now, mother—I'm only going down to the flat below.'

She glanced at him curiously. Recently his visits there had been more frequent. He stayed later, too, and she wondered if he were always welcome. She knew instinctively that he could have nothing in common with either Miss Harding or Rose O'Daly, yet, with a mother's intuition she guessed that her son was attracted by Rose.

She had seen the girl on several occasions, admired her, noticed her frocks, her perfect style of dressing, her pretty French mannerisms and turns of speech. She had not spoken much to her, it was with Nora that she had grown so friendly since the death of Hugh. Forgetting the true adage that tells how extremes meet, Anne had been surprised that George should be attracted by a type so opposite to his own. Yet it was hardly a matter for surprise. He had never before met a girl like Rose, a woman like Nora. He knew that his mother was a 'lady' but the knowledge had meant little to him, in fact, he would have preferred that his mother had been a woman of the people. With his Communistic ideals, it did not seem fair that she should belong by birth to that class which he was for ever inveighing. Reason might have told him that Rose O'Daly would have no sympathy with his ideas, she had, indeed, openly said that she was definitely anti-Communistic, and he knew that Nora Harding hated his doctrines.

But when did a young man in love ever reason? Reason, logic, philosophy—all go overboard then. This was the case with George, yet, as Hope stays when Reason has fled, he beguiled himself with the delusion that he would win Rose for his wife. If she wished it, he would even marry her in a church, against his principles though such a proceeding would be. She was usually kind to him; at times only a trifle impatient. Truth to tell, he bored her terribly, and only her good manners prevented her from showing this more openly. George, blind, infatuated, had no idea of this, but his mother, seeing deeper into the girl's heart, noting her absolute indifference to all that concerned George, knew better than he did, and knew, too, that disillusionment awaited him.

Except, of course, that the girl, with the innate thriftiness and common sense of the Frenchwoman towards marriage—and Anne realised that Rose O'Daly was more French than Irish—might be inclined to consider George's proposal more favourably now that he was heir to the Ballafagh estate.

Anne had not spoken to her son about the matter yet. Nothing was certain about it. For one thing, there might be other children born to her brother, but George was heir at the present moment. Indeed only that morning she had received a letter from Victor, drawing her attention to the fact, and telling her that he would be in Dublin for a few days soon, and would come and see her, and make the acquaintance of his nephew; Victor had added the pregnant words 'and heir', after nephew, and those two words had decided her to speak to her son.

How would he take it? He, the Communist, the advocate of equality for all men, the wager of war against all Capitalists— amongst which class he ranked landed gentry as the worst offenders. Would he agree to take his place, to do his duty, as Hewdon of Ballafagh? Still more, how would he stand with the 'county?' Poor Anne, remembering the 'county set' of her girlhood, in the early years of the present century, felt her face flush with shame. Thinking of her son's accent, his *gauche* manners, his absolute ignorance of all those things which meant so much to those amidst whom she had been reared, she could have wept her heart out. When Victor saw his nephew what would he think—what in the world would he think? Her stupid act of folly had come home to her now.

But the consequences must be faced. She had better speak to George now, for her brother might arrive any day.

'George,' she said, 'can you spare me a few moments? I want to speak to you.'

'Of course, mother. What is it?'

He came over and sat down beside her as he spoke. That was one redeeming feature which he possessed. He was always kind and polite to her; not all the Rationalistic doctrines which he had imbibed could make him rude to his mother, or cause him to treat her with any less respect than he had done when, as a little fellow, he attended the big Board School in the East End.

'George,' she said, 'have you thought that the death of your cousin Hugh has made a great difference to you?'

'To me? In what way?'

'You are now your uncle's heir.'

'My uncle's heir. You mean——?'

'I mean that if my brother were to die you would succeed to Ballafagh House and the estate.'

'Ballafagh? The house where you were born? You mean that it would belong to me—the land—everything?'

'Yes.'

'But I would never take it—never go there!'

'What would you do?'

'Sell it and give the proceeds to the Cause. Better still, turn it into a Holiday Home for our workers, a sort of Headquarters for Ireland.'

'George!'

The cry of anguish. Ballafagh. Her dear old home; so dignified, so stately; beautiful within doors and without. That it should be put to such use!

'You could not do it!' she cried, 'you dare not! George—think for one moment of all my people who have been born, lived, died there—from one generation to another! And the pictures—the silver—the furniture, all heirlooms, added to through the centuries! You would leave them there for the use of common, uncultivated men, or else sell them to strangers, who would appreciate them only for their monetary value—to whom they mean simply pounds, shillings, pence. Jews would come and barter for them, and resell them at a profit. My son—you are a Hewdon after all. You could not—you dare not—do this thing!'

It was Anne Hewdon who spoke. She had forgotten that she had ever been the wife of Patrick Dempsey. All the traditions of her race called to her; the blood of her ancestors raced in her veins.

Her son stared at her.

'Well, it's what I intend to do if I ever own this old place. Surely you don't expect me to give up my whole life's work, to turn traitor to those in whose service I am. Do you expect me to leave my own class and join those whom I hate and despise? Join the class which has fattened upon our people—sweated them—paid them starvation wages for centuries? become an Irish landlord—you must be mad even to think of such a thing!'

Anne was staring out of the window, her heart frozen within her. The miserable expression in her tired eyes hurt her son. What a pity he thought, that they could never see things in the same light—but they never would.

'I'm sorry, mother,' he said, 'we must only agree to differ.'

Then, as she did not speak. 'I must go now. I will be going round to the rooms later on, so don't sit up for me.'

He put his arms round her shoulders and kissed her cheek. It was cold and unresponsive to his caress, and George swore softly as he went down the stairs to the flat below.

'The cursed inheritance of an effete class! Their prejudices, traditions, family pride, and all the rest! Rotten abominations—out of date rubbish! They need a lesson—and will get it!'

Being quite at home in Nora's flat, he opened the door leading into the tiny hall, and called out:

'Hello! Anyone at home?'

Even as he spoke, the door of the sittingroom flew open, and Rose—such a Rose as he had surely never seen before—burst upon his vision. He could not have told how she was dressed, he only saw a pink frock with frills, he had not noticed the dainty stockings to match, and the pretty shoes. He knew that her hair was shining, her eyes sparkling, and her face more lovely than he had ever seen it before. Could it be that he had taken her by surprise? That she was glad to see him—that it was he who had brought the colour to her cheeks, the light to her eyes?

So delighted with his own imaginings was he, that he did not observe the blank expression of disappointment which had overshadowed Rose's face when she saw who it was.

'Oh, Mr Dempsey—it's you——'

'Yes, May I come in? I hope I'm not intruding?'

At last he felt a chill in the air, and once more that wretched sense of inferiority seized upon him. How often he had experienced the feeling when meeting with people of a different class than himself. Not that he considered himself inferior; he most certainly did not. Still he could not help the feeling, furious though it made him. And now, as he entered the room, it gripped him again, so that he knew he was stooping badly, and stumbled awkwardly over a footstool. Yet he did not see that Rose was wishing him far away. Generally a shrewd observer, this evening he was blind to all save the beauty of the woman he loved.

'Is Miss Harding out?'

'Yes. She has gone to see a friend.'

Rose could have added that Nora had had the grace to make herself scarce on this momentous occasion. 'But then, poor imbecile, he does not know that Antoine is coming,' she thought, 'I had better give him a hint or he will stay here for hours.'

'I am expecting a friend from Paris,' she said, 'he will arrive at any moment now.'

The glance she gave the clock as if to say: 'Oh, hurry—hurry on—make the minutes fly!' the light that came into her eyes when she spoke, roused him, so that a sudden fury of jealousy possessed him. She had said that 'he' was coming. It was a man then. What man? A lover?

'Is he an old friend?'

He could hardly articulate, the words seemed to choke him.

'Oh, yes—we have known each other for years.'

He could make nothing from her words; perhaps after all it was nothing. Yet, if the friendship were renewed it might grow into something deeper. And a Frenchman, too. He had all the prejudices of the untravelled, insular Englishman with regard to 'foreigners', for it must be remembered that his education and environment had been English entirely; his mother had never helped to make him Irish in his outlook, and for his father he had always had a great contempt, and unconsciously modelled all Irish on that pattern.

Suddenly, without giving himself time to think, he rushed headlong into speech.

'Rose!' he cried, 'I love you—I love you! You must know I do? Will you marry me?'

Then, as she sat looking at him in petrified silence, he went on: 'I know you do not see things from my point of view—but if we love each other what does it matter? Indeed, if you wish it very much I will marry you in your own church.'

There was no reply for a moment. Rose was trying to collect herself, to understand his words. Was it possible that this so vulgar little Cockney, this terrible bore, whom Nora had taken compassion on, as she sometimes did on the stray mongrels nosing round the Square—was he actually asking her to marry him? Yes— there he sat, as serious as a judge; anxious too, under his quiet exterior; she knew that by the expression of his eyes. But how absurd—how ridiculous it all was! As if she—she who was to marry Antoine—would ever look at this poor creature. Besides, there was the religious aspect, his Communistic aims—all anathema to Rose O'Daly, whose mother was descended from the minor nobility of France, and whose father was a good Irish Catholic.

For the moment an almost irresistible desire to laugh overcame her, but she pulled herself together. That would never do, and anyway she must try and get rid of him quietly—and finally—before the arrival of Antoine. Neither did she wish to hurt his feelings. He knew no better; his impertinence was due to ignorance. As if she would ever look at this little Cockney—she, Rose O'Daly, who had always a following of men from artistic and literary circles, and could choose whom she would. And then the thought of what Antoine would say if he every heard of this wonderful proposal! Oh! if she did not get rid of him soon, she would most certainly disgrace herself by laughter.

'I am sorry—'

But he broke in upon her words.

'Don't say anything yet—think it over for a little while.'

The pronunciation of the words jarred upon her afresh, so that she replied curtly: 'There is no need for me to do so. As I was about to say, I am sorry if you have allowed yourself to—to like me. I did not encourage you to do so—that you know. It is my fiancé who comes this evening—I am affianced already, so you will understand——'

A sudden noise in the hall, footsteps approaching. With a little cry she sprang to her feet.

'Ah—but he is here—he has arrived! Please—you will now go?'

She flew to the door and opened it. A man stood on the threshold, dark, not too tall, perfectly attired according to the French fashions. In fact, a typical Parisian of the better class, had but George known that type. He saw him bend to kiss Rose's hand, heard her rapturous cry of 'Antoine—*c'est toi!*' and his murmured '*Chérie!*' and then, with rage and hatred in his heart, with his world rocking round him, George stumbled to his feet, passed into the hall, and out into the street.

CHAPTER XV

VICTOR REMEMBERS

A few days later, Victor Hewdon stood before the door of his sister's flat in George Square. During the train journey from Mayo, he had been thinking—and rather dreading—the coming interview.

What would Anne be like after all these years? He remembered, as if it were but yesterday—so deeply had the affair been engraved on his memory—the morning when she had run away from home with the gardener's boy. He could still see the worried face of Michael Brennan, standing in front of him, twisting his old hat in his hands, trying to tell him that Miss Anne was gone—gone with Pat Dempsey. He remembered the time that followed; his mother's agony of mind, her humiliation; the gossip of the servants; the curious glances thrown in his direction when he rode into Larramore; the different way in which his own circle had received the news; some of them pitying him, others laughing, sneering; and some almost glad, rejoicing to see the Hewdon pride laid low at last. Yes—it had been a wretched time. And now he supposed it was going to be revived again.

Twenty-one years ago.

Again he wondered what Anne would be like. As far as he knew she had only written once to Ballafagh House, Saying they had been married in Liverpool; after that—to his knowledge—she had never written again.

Then his own marriage. It was Anne who had been the indirect cause of that; his sister's conduct had turned him against all who were not of his own class, and, in some extraordinary way had caused him to vow that his wife should be of his own religion, his own class. His sister had turned traitor to all the traditions in which they had both been reared; he would not follow her example. So he had written the letter to the woman whom he loved so dearly—loved as he would never love another—written it in the white heat of the moment, fearful that his love might make him weak. During the miserable time that followed, he had one consolation—he had pleased his mother. She was not slow to take advantage of his attitude, and had arranged his marriage with the daughter of Lord Larramore. How beautiful Aileen had been, and how strange it was that she could never stir his pulse, never move him to love or admiration. His whole heart had been given to another, and he had no love left for his wife. Respect he gave her, honouring her as the mistress of Ballafagh, the mother of his son. Yet, between them there seemed always to be a high wall—impassable to both.

He had been glad when the European war had come. He joined up at once, and rejoiced in the excitement, the danger, of those days. Only for his mother, he would not have cared had he been killed, but he escaped with a slight wound. Escaped to take part in a war that was ever more dreadful in his eyes, a war in which brother fought against brother, father against son.

Victor Hewdon had offered his services to the Free State forces, considering that it was his duty to do so. His mother had died the year before; Hugh was in Trinity; Aileen, as far as he knew, was indifferent. She had never let him know her opinions about National questions, he was so bitter on the other side, and she felt it would do more harm than good. That his son would ever dream of joining the 'Irregulars', never for a moment entered Victor's head. But he had joined them, and his father had given the order to fire, the fatal order which had sent Hugh to his death. In giving the order he had but done his duty, done what that low bounder who was the CO at Margallin Barracks, had ordered him to do. He was to fire on any suspicious looking car or lorry which he saw passing. Why, in Heaven's name, had not that man, when riding past on a motor bicycle a short time before, told him that he was going to arrest some Irregulars who had been detained on the bridge outside the town? He had not done so. Hence the terrible mistake.

And Aileen. Never would the memory of her eyes when he had told her leave his thoughts. The eyes of a stricken deer. She had not reproached him, he would rather that she had, but had just faded steadily from that day. Now, but a few weeks after, she was a shadow of her old self; she, who had been so young looking for her years, had aged quickly; her lovely face was lined, silver ran amid the thick brown hair; the beautiful eyes were weary from weeping. She did not eat, spoke but little, was always gentle.

The death of his son revealed to Victor that his wife had been in sympathy with the 'Irregulars', that, indeed, she had always been a 'rebel' at heart. Hardly could he credit it, but her words when he told her of Hugh's death—'Thank God it was for Ireland!' told him all.

Aileen had shed no tears at first. Her husband, coming to Ballafagh to break the news to her, had not known how to tell her; how to explain that Hugh had been with the 'Irregulars', and that he—his father—had given the order to the firing party which had resulted in the boy's death. But she had listened quietly, calmly, and he discovered that she had known that Hugh was in the fight in Dublin. He had managed to get a letter through to her during the first few days of the fight; after that she had heard nothing, and had been eating her heart out in anxiety, watching, waiting, praying. She told Victor this, and he stared at her aghast.

'But you, Aileen—you dared—you taught him these rebel doctrines!'

'Yes, I taught them.'

'To my son?'

'To MY son.'

'You dared to do it!'

For a moment he had even forgotten his sorrow, his loss. He could only remember that his wife—the wife of Hewdon, of Ballafagh—had made a 'rebel' of his son.

'There was little need to teach him—to influence him, in any way,' she went on, 'he was Irish of the Irish always; his every thought was for his country—for her freedom. From a child he loved to read, to learn about those who died as he has done—for Ireland. I am lonely, bereft, desolate, but I thank God I can say that I am proud of my son!'

Victor said no more; he looked upon her as distraught—mad. He would not torment her now; afterwards she might feel differently. They spoke little about Hugh after that. Aileen kept to her own rooms and the garden, walking up and down the paths where she and Hugh had so often strolled together; going for walks in the woods, or by the river where the boy had been wont to go fishing with the Flynns. She remembered old Tony and his words to her in 1916: 'I may not see it, gracious lady—but you will!'

'He was wrong,' she thought, 'once more we have tried and failed again. This time through the treachery of our own—and that is the worst of all!'

It was over a month before Victor mentioned his sister to her.

'Aileen,' he said one evening, coming to her room after dinner, 'may I stay and talk to you for a few minutes?'

'Why, of course, Victor.'

Glancing at her, he noticed how thin she was growing, how worn, above all, how much older looking. His wife had always been so youthful for her age. Hugh had been tremendously proud of his lovely young mother. But now she looked her full age and more.

'You are not looking well,' he said, suddenly, 'would you care to go somewhere for a change?'

'No, thank you, I am quite well. I hope,' with wistful smile, 'that you have not come to talk about my health?'

'No. I just noticed that you were not looking well, that is all. What I wanted to speak to you about was the difference that—that the death of Hugh makes in the family. With regard to the next heir.'

He found it difficult to explain especially as it was quite apparent that she had never considered the matter.

'The next heir?'

'Yes. The heir to Ballafagh now is the son of my sister Anne. Did you ever hear of her?'

Anne had been a forbidden subject when he had married Aileen, and he had not mentioned her to his wife. But she replied now:

'Yes. Your mother mentioned her once or twice. She said little, but I gathered that she had made an unfortunate marriage.'

'Unfortunate? Terrible! She ran away with the boy who helped in the gardens—one Patrick Dempsey. He was younger than she was, and just a rough labouring lad. We heard afterwards that he had been an inmate of an industrial school. The whole thing was frightful. My mother suffered abominably—I will never forget it.'

'And your sister—is she alive?'

'Yes, she is in Dublin now, and her son, George, is with her.'

'How did you hear?'

He flushed slightly, but she did not notice.

'I met a Miss Harding who was District Nurse here when Anne ran away. She told me. She was in the van when—when Hugh was shot.'

'Was she a prisoner, too?'

'Yes.'

'Oh, I am glad she was with him! Was she with him—all the time?'

'All the time. She was kind beyond words. He died in her arms.'

'Oh, how I should like to meet her—to thank her!'

'She lives in Dublin—works there as Public Health Nurse. She happens to be in the same house as Anne, and so told me about her.'

'I see. And your nephew. What is he like?'

'I have not the faintest idea. He was brought up in London, and I believe they were very poor. However, I am sure that Anne has done her best to instil some decent instincts into him; she will have tried to counteract his father's influence. I say this, because I feel perfectly certain that once her infatuation was over—and it would not last for long—Anne would repent her criminal folly every day of her life. There is a girl, too, but I understand that she is married in London. You will not mind, Aileen, if I bring Anne and the young fellow here for a visit? Not just now, but later on.'

'Bring them whenever you like. Why not let them come at once? They are your nearest relatives now. I wonder would Miss Harding come and see us too? I would so like to thank her for her kindness to Hugh.'

'Oh, no—I do not think she would come! She is kept very busy at her work.'

Aileen looked at him as he spoke. She thought that his objection—for she knew he did object—to Miss Harding as a visitor, was on account of her political views. She resolved not to make a point of having her now. Perhaps later she might come.

So it happened that shortly afterwards, Victor Hewdon arrived at the flat in George Square, and rang the bell for admittance.

The door was opened by a middle-aged woman, thin, unprepossessing, with lines of worry deeply engraved upon her face.

'Is Mrs Dempsey at home?'

Then something about the woman standing in the doorway made him pause. Was it her eyes? A fleeting expression passing over her face? Whatever it was, he exclaimed:

'Anne! Is it you?'

'And you are Victor. Come in—I did not expect you so soon.' He followed her into the sittingroom, trying to realise the fact that this woman, old, worn, was his sister. He remembered her when she was so different. Not that she had ever been a beauty—as poor Pat Dempsey had sometimes said to himself—but she had been young, buoyant, full of life; there had been times too when she had looked very well, especially when riding or driving. It was twenty-one years since he had met her, twenty-one years of a woman's life, the years, too, that make the most difference; but even allowing for that, she had aged beyond all recognition. He glanced involuntarily at her workworn hands, and noticing his dismay, she smiled grimly.

'You see a change in me, I suppose?'

'I do. You must have gone through a terrible lot of trouble. Why did you not write, and let us know how things were with you?'

'I wrote twice. Once when I was on the verge of starvation—just after Mary was born—and again later when I was badly in want of money for the rent. But the letters were not answered.'

'To whom did you write?'

'To you first, and then to mother.'

'I did not receive mine. I would have replied had I done so.'

'I always thought you did not get the letter. Mother must have kept it from you.'

'I am sorry. Tell me all now, Anne. I have so often wondered where you were, and how things were with you.'

She told him something of the past years, not everything; her pride would not allow her to speak of her husband's drinking habits, of the sordid surroundings of their East End home, of her daughter's marriage. But he read between the lines and understood more than she intended that he should. Then came the question which she had been expecting, waiting for—and dreading.

'And my nephew, Anne? What is the boy like? I hope he is likely to do credit to the old name. As you know, he is now my heir, and in all human probability will be master of Ballafagh when I am gone.

'But you are comparatively young, Victor. There may be other children born to you. Anyway, you should live for many a year yet.'

He shook his head.

'George is my heir, and it is my wish that he be recognised as such. I had hoped to see him this evening.'

'So you will. He is out. You know we are poor, and he has to work. He has a — a position here now.'

'What does he work at? Is he literary?'

'He writes a little. But he is devoted to reading.'

'The library at Ballafagh will appeal to him then. What particular job is he at now?'

'He is a representative—an agent——'

'Oh, a traveller! Well, we must change all that. The heir to Ballafagh must not go round the country looking for orders for commercial firms. We are hoping—Aileen and myself—that you will both come back with me to Ballafagh for a visit. In fact, we should like you to make it your home for the future. Aileen is lonely. Mother and aunt are dead, and now Hugh is gone. She was wrapped up in the boy—they were everything to one another. I would be so glad if you and she became friends. And then George must learn something of the estate.

'Surely, Victor, all that is time enough! You talk as if you were going to die tomorrow.'

'Have you forgotten how our father died? Did we expect it so soon? Did I think that I would be called to leave my studies in Dublin and come to take up my responsibilities as the owner of Ballafagh? I wish my heir to get into touch with the tenants, and get to understand the working of the estate.'

'The same old pedantic Victor!' Anne thought to herself. But she also wondered what she should say to him about George—how to prepare him for the meeting with his nephew. What a shock it would be for her brother! She had better say something, for it was plain to be seen that Victor was expecting to meet a young fellow of his own class, with similar ideas and opinions.

'George is very like you in appearance,' she said, 'extraordinarily like you. But you know, he has been brought up in England, he is very English is his outlook——'

He interrupted her quickly.

'He is none the worse for that! I am extremely glad to hear you say so. Nowadays, this rebel nonsense is destroying the Youth of our country, why even Hugh——'

He paused for a moment and glanced at her.

'You have heard about Hugh, of course?'

'Oh, yes—don't you know he stayed here for some days?'

'I had forgotten. Well, you can imagine the blow all that was to me. To think that a Hewdon——. Ah Well, I am glad that there will be no fear of anything of that sort with my nephew.'

'No, there will be no fear of that. But——'

Even while she hesitated, not knowing how to go on, they both heard the key turn in the door, and the next moment George Dempsey entered the room.

CHAPTER XVI

VICTOR MEETS HIS NEPHEW

'This is George now——George, your Uncle Victor.'

Anne Dempsey felt far from happy as she made her relations known to each other. Uncle and nephew shook hands, and then took stock of one another.

Victor saw a young man, absurdly like what he had been himself at the same age, as far as features, hair, colouring, went. But there the resemblance ceased. This boy held himself badly, and Victor's opinion was that he had never been drilled, and was in need of much physical culture; he wore the wrong clothes in the wrong way, his manners were *gauche*, his movements awkward. But it was when George spoke that Victor got the shock of his life. Never for one moment had he imagined that the boy would speak so badly. What had Anne been thinking about to allow him to develop such an accent? Still, the boy was his nephew, and now, unfortunately, his heir. He must only try and make the best of it. After all these were but outward defects; the boy might be good at heart, willing to learn. Perhaps a private tutor——

'Well, my boy, I'm glad to meet you. I expect your mother will have spoken to you about me?'

'Yes, lately. I did not know of your existence until recently.'

'Thinks he was neglected, I suppose. Imagines he is independent, while being simply rude.' So thought Victor to himself. Aloud he said:

'We will agree to let bygones be bygones. I have been talking to your mother, and it is settled that you both come back with me to Ballafagh for a visit, and indeed, your Aunt Aileen and myself hope that you will make it your home, that you and your mother will live there for the future. You know you are now my heir, and I want you to understand the work of the estate——'

'Thank you,' George interrupted, coldly, 'but I do not wish to visit your home. If ever I own the place it will no longer be an "estate", as you call it, and it will be managed very differently from what it is at present.'

Major Hewdon stared helplessly at his nephew. Was he mad? He glanced at his sister to see if she could unravel the puzzle, but poor Anne refused to meet his eye. What she had been dreading had come at last. Still she might try to stop George from going too far.

'George,' she said, 'your uncle is not interested in your opinions. He has kindly asked us on a visit, and I hope you will come with me. I should like you to see my old home.'

'And I would not like to see it. You know, mother, that I would do a lot to please you, but not this. I wish to forget that you ever belonged to the Capitalist class, and especially to that worst class of all—the Irish landowner.' He turned then to his uncle and went on: 'You do not seem to understand that I am here as a Communist organiser, trying to wake up the Irish people, trying to get them to understand the ideals for which we stand. Over here, they know nothing of the Brotherhood of Man, the international work for universal equality. They are imbued with rubbish about Faith and Fatherland—all that rot! I have uphill work, but I am doing my best. As to visiting Ballafagh, meeting more people of the class against whom we are fighting—I will not do so. If ever I own the place it will be used as a Communist Headquarters in Ireland.'

His mother interrupted him suddenly, angrily.

'Stop! We have had enough of such talk. Your uncle is not interested in it—and neither am I!'

He stared at her in astonishment. This was a new attitude for his mother to adopt. In his own mind, he called it 'the fine lady stunt'.

To say that Victor Hewdon was stupefied would only be fact. Hardly could he believe the evidence of his own ears, of his senses.

'Good God!' he burst forth, and for him to use any kind of strong language was a sign that he was terribly moved: 'Is it possible that I have heard aright? Is it possible that one who has Hewdon blood in his veins—who is—God help us—heir to our home, that he should stand there and preach the cursed doctrine of Communism? Anne—did you know of this?'

'You need not blame me,' she replied, 'and perhaps he is not entirely to blame himself. He was born in poverty—the sordid poverty of the East End of London—and had to go to work when he was fifteen in a boot factory. He gave up his religion, and listened to the pernicious doctrines taught by demagogues at every street corner over there. I did my best, but he was beyond me.' She broke down suddenly, and wept bitterly.

George had seldom seen his mother shed a tear; he hated to see her do so now, and had they been alone, would have put his arms round her, trying to comfort her. But there was this uncle of his still planted there, not seemingly inclined to move. He would go out himself and leave the two of them. He had a meeting at the 'Rooms' that night, and so could find an excuse.

'I am due at a meeting in our Rooms—I must ask you to excuse me.'

He rose awkwardly from his seat and left the room, and they heard him go down the stairs, and out of the house. Wretchedly lonely, with sullen anger in his heart, he walked towards the meeting place of his organisation, while, for the first time, a feeling of doubt, a realisation of the futility of his mission, entered his soul.

Brother and sister were silent for a few minutes after he had left them. Then Victor took a chair beside Anne, and laid his hand on hers. As he did so, he noticed, with pity, how roughened and coarse it was.

'My poor Anne,' he said, 'this is terrible! Why did you not tell me what to expect?'

'I was ashamed,' she whispered through her tears. 'Oh Victor, I dreaded the meeting between you both. George is so hot—so bitter!'

'What work exactly is he doing here? Do you know?'

'What he told you, I think. Those people for whom he works seem to be in touch with the Soviet Government, but he tells me little. And he is a good boy—a good son only for those wrong ideas. I blame myself in part. I was not a good Catholic for many years—all during his childhood and early boyhood, I was careless, and so gave him no example. And his poor father—Mary, thank God, is so different.'

'You cannot expect me to be glad that you are a Roman Catholic,' replied her brother, 'but I must admit that from the standpoint of a Christian gentleman—which I hope I am—I would rather that my heir were a Roman—and a rebel to boot—than a Communist. The very name stinks in the nostrils of all decent people! Look at Russia today! The misery of the unfortunate people, the massacres committed, the tyranny—— Oh, well, it's no use talking. The question is what can we do? Do you think there is any hope at all that we may yet make a decent man of him? Could we get him down to Ballafagh by any means?'

'I am afraid not. Ballafagh and all that it stands for, is anathema to him. Lately, too—this is in confidence—he has had trouble of his own. He fell in love with a girl in the flat below us—Rose O'Daly—a most fascinating little creature, half Irish, half French, a journalist——'

'Oh, I have met her! Was she not with—with Miss Harding when they were taken in custody, the time that——'

She saw he could not mention that time without emotion, and said quickly, 'Yes, that is she. She was engaged already to a Frenchman, but George did not know, and asked her to marry him. He felt the whole thing terribly, more especially as he never cared for any other woman—never took the slightest interest in one, always saying that he was wedded to the Cause. He felt it so badly that I was half afraid he would do something desperate.'

'Would she have any influence with him?'

'Hardly now—at least I do not think so.'

'I want to get him to Ballafagh. I have an idea that his Hewdon blood would call to him, if only we had him there. Anne—it is worth trying. We must fight for the sake of Ballafagh and its future.'

'And for the sake of George himself.'

Before they could say more a knock at the door interrupted them. Anne called out 'come in', and the next moment Nora Harding stood on the threshold. She changed colour when she saw Victor. Had she known he would be there at that hour, she would not have come up from her own flat.

'Oh, Miss Harding, come in! This is my brother, Major Hewdon, I think you have met before? At Margallin, was it not?'

The eyes of the man and woman met for one fleeting glance. Yes—they had met before. Met in a world of Youth and Romance—a thousand years ago.

Nora was the first to recover herself.

'I am glad to meet you again, Major Hewdon,' she said.

'And I you. How are you feeling now? Have you quite got over the effects of your ordeal at Margallin?'

She laughed.

'Yes—quite! But we had a nasty time when we were prisoners in the barracks.'

She and the other girls have been detained for a week in the military barracks at Margallin, and had gone through a most unpleasant time until they were released and allowed to return to

Dublin. Dr Givor and the men had been removed to another town, and it was many months before they met Nora Harding again. At the present moment, she had not the slightest idea as to where they were imprisoned.

To Rose O'Daly, her term of imprisonment was just fun; she kept up the spirits of the others, and when released, managed to send a full account of it all to her paper in Paris.

'I thought George was here,' said Nora, 'I had a message for him.'

'No,' replied Anne, 'he has gone out.' Then, some impulse made her say: 'Miss Harding, my brother is interested in George. You see he is his heir now, and he wishes to persuade him to go on a visit to Ballafagh. You know George's ideas and opinions, he has refused. But we think that if he could be got there——'

She paused, wondering whether it was wise to take Nora into their confidence. Although she had only spoken of their meeting at Margallin Anne knew something of that old love story. She had not heard much, but still her mother had made some remarks to her at the time. However, her own foolish escapade had intervened, and she had almost forgotten about it. Now the story came back to her. Victor was already adding his words to hers, explaining how much he wanted his nephew to see Ballafagh—to realise that it would be his one day.

'My sister spoke of Miss O'Daly. We were discussing the point as to whether she would have any influence now with my nephew. Do you think she could persuade him to go to Ballafagh?'

'I think she could do more that way than anyone else,' Nora replied. 'Rose is one of the most irresistible of mortals—when she chooses. I quite understand that George may feel sore in that direction, in fact I know he does, but I still think she could talk him over.'

'How would it be if you asked Miss O'Daly for a visit, too? And perhaps Miss Harding?'

Anne had not wanted to ask Nora, but she felt that she could hardly suggest Rose alone. Nora flushed and said hastily: 'I am afraid I could not go—I am very busy just now.'

'Why can you not go? And your holidays next week?'

It was Rose herself, who, according to her way, had knocked and entered at that one moment. Victor looking at her did not wonder at his nephew's infatuation, for she was a dazzling little creature.

She came over to him now, hand outstretched, and he bent and kissed it French fashion.

'That is nice of you, Major Hewdon,' she said, 'so seldom here one finds the polite manner.'

'We were just speaking of you,' he said, 'and you see it is a case of hearing your wings—and seeing yourself.'

'And what were you saying?—Something bad, of course.'

'No—nothing but what was good. And now we want you to do something good for us—to help us if you can in a very particular way.'

She looked at him curiously, her laughing eyes serious for a moment. Then she said: 'I will help you anyway I can—if Nora wishes it.'

'I do wish it, Rose.'

'Then you may speak but to command!' Rose replied in her usual gay voice.

'That is a promise?' asked Victor.

'It is a promise.'

CHAPTER XVII

THE PROMISE

The month of October can be beautiful in the country. Given dry roads, weather not too cold, yet with a nip of frost morning and evening, the hedges and trees decked out in all their autumnal colours, and the chestnuts falling at our feet—a country walk on such a day is a sheer joy.

These days had come to Mayo that late autumn, and to those who had been for long 'in city pent', the beauty around them was a revelation. The gardens at Ballafagh were gay with late flowers, and the roses—those last roses of summer which bloom in October as if to mock us for calling them June flowers—were particularly lovely.

At Ballafagh House, on a certain afternoon, a group of people were assembled for tea in Mrs Hewdon's room. It was a delightful room, and Aileen had furnished and decorated it according to her own taste. In that room Hugh and she had been wont to sit and talk by the firelight, and for some time after his death she could hardly bear that anyone else should share it with her. But she was making an effort to overcome all that, to be friendly and sociable with her guests. She was not strong lately, and this afternoon lay on a couch drawn near to the cheery log fire. Rose O'Daly was seated on a low stool in the middle of the hearthrug, Nora on a chair beside Aileen, while George and his mother occupied seats on the opposite side of the fireplace.

The four had returned to Ballafagh House with Victor as he had wished. Rose, by some method of her own, had persuaded George to be of the party. At first he had been supposed to come only for a few days, but several weeks had gone by, and he was still there, and although Nora would have to return to her work in another week, he had made no allusion to going back to Dublin with her.

Rose, as usual was chatting away, while Nora and Aileen put in a word now and then. Anne was silent for the most part. The contrast between this room and those awful places where she had had to live and work, the lovely gowns worn by her sister-in-law, her beautiful hands, so different from her own workworn ones—all this had made her depressed, miserable. Although she knew that she had only herself to blame for the tragedy of her life, still the contrast was bitter. George was silent, too. Since coming to Balla-fagh he had been acutely conscious of his accent, manners—everything. Not that he had met any of those people with whom he had been ready to fight; neither had his new relations let him see by the slightest sign, that they noticed either his manners or accent. He just realised it—that was all.

Sitting, moody, occupied with his own thoughts, he did not notice at first that the others had finished tea and gone out of the room, leaving him alone with his aunt.

'Are they all gone?' he asked, then.

'Yes—all have deserted me except yourself. Come and sit on this stool beside me, and let us have a little talk.'

The dusk was upon the room, which was lit only by the gleam from the fire, shining on the great bowls of chrysanthemums and late roses, on the silver of the tea table, the etchings on the walls. George involuntarily gave a sigh of appreciation as he took the seat beside Aileen. A month ago, he could not have believed that he would care for such things, would have thought it his duty to sneer at them, to fight them as things representing the spirit of Capitalism.

They had talked before, the two of them, sitting by the fire like this. At first, it had been pain for Aileen, reminding her of those dear days spent with Hugh, but now she had come to love George for his own sake.

As for him, she had cast a spell over him. She seemed to him like some spirit inhabiting, for a brief space, a human body. This made it hard for him to continue to believe that Death was the end of all things, and that her spirit, soul, call it what he might, would die with her body of clay. There was, to George Dempsey, a something, an essence, that was immortal about this woman. And she had been so kind to him, so friendly.

He loved his mother deeply, but she did not understand him. Aileen in her quiet way was better able to fathom the depths of his character. She seemed young to him, he could never remember that she was but a few years younger than his mother. He and Aileen were more like brother and sister than aunt and nephew.

'Were you out today?' she asked.

'Yes, I went for a walk—oh, for miles! The country is beautiful—I never knew how beautiful before. Do you know, Aunt Aileen, that when my father was dying his last words were: 'Thanks be to God I can see the green fields again!' I did not know then what he meant—what Whitechapel must have been to him—but now that I have seen where he lived—I understand.'

'And you will understand better as you know the country and its people better,' she replied, 'you will have a great responsibility one day. Do you ever think how great it will be?'

'You mean?'

'I mean all this land—although the estate is not big now—the tenants, the people who work for you. It will be your duty when you are Master of Hewdon to see to their happiness and well-being.'

George was silent, and Aileen went on: 'You have talked about bad landlords, and unfortunately there have been many such in Ireland. But not all of them. We have but a small estate it's true, but all our people are happy.'

'But Aunt Aileen I have told you that if ever I own this place—I hope that won't be for years and years—I mean to change everything. It will be run on different lines entirely.'

'You mean——'

'As a Communistic Headquarters for the West of Ireland—a place where the Irish people will learn what our aim is—what Communism means, what it really stands for. Each man should be given an equal share of the land which would be worked and tilled for the common good——'

'Forgive me for being rude, but my dear boy, you are talking the greatest rubbish! You would simply be asking for trouble if you tried that here.'

'But if we lived under Communistic rules——'

She laughed gently and ran her fingers through his hair, as he sat beside her on the low stool.

'Please don't talk about such things,' she said, 'I do not like them. Won't you tell me more about Hugh?'

During those days which had elapsed between the return to the flat in George Square and the journey to Margallin George Dempsey had grown to know and like Hugh. He had often spoken of him to his mother, telling her how brave he was, how impressed he had been, almost in spite of himself, by the boy's ideals and love of country.

'I got so fond of him,' he said, and then he added rather shame-facedly, 'I suppose there is some truth in the saying that "blood is thicker than water".'

'Why, of course.'

She laid her hand gently on his, and he wondered anew at its whiteness—too, white, almost transparent, had he but known it.

Having him beside her there in the firelight, she could talk more freely to him than at any other time, and it was then that she tried to inculcate into him—this boy who was so alien to her in every way—some of the ideals which she had taught to her son. But it was difficult work. George was imbued with false ideas, he had been fed on garbage for mind and soul, he viewed the world from wrong angles, and Aileen's task was hard. Still, she thought that she was making a little progress. If only she could make a lasting impression on him, sow a few seeds that would one day blossom into fruit. There was one thing which she had been wanting to say to him for some time now, but had put it off from day to day. Suddenly, she determined to speak:

'I have wished to tell you something—to prepare you——

She paused, and George glanced at her curiously. As she did not go on, he asked, 'Yes—what is it, Aunt Aileen?'

She told him then, speaking in quiet matter of fact tones, telling him that the doctor had given her but a short while longer to live. At first he did not believe her, could not credit it, but as she went more fully into details, he realised that she was speaking plain fact. He gazed at her, stupefied.

'Do not look like that,' she said, 'surely you know that I will be glad to go? Since Hugh left me, my life has been so empty, so desolate, that it has not been worth living. I am only speaking the literal truth. In telling you, I did not want to distress you, and I do not want you to think too much about it, but I do want you to try and see things more from the point of view of the rest of your family. Don't think that every one who belongs to our class in life—the class to which your mother and uncle and myself all belong—are all by nature bad and selfish. We are not indeed, and the older you get the more convinced you will be that there are good and bad in every walk of life—and that most of us are just a decent grey—neither very black nor very white.'

He hardly heard her words, so grieved was he by what she had told him. That she was going to die! Going where he would never see her again. That lovely, gracious body to soon be food for worms. Corruption and all its horrors. In spite of himself he envied now the great Christian cry of triumph over Death:

> *I know that my Redeemer liveth,*
> *And that He shall stand up at the last upon the earth;*
> *And after my skin hath been thus destroyed,*
> *Yet from my flesh I shall see God.*

A wonderful, beautiful belief. And the absolute certainty which those words conveyed to one. Absolute knowledge. Not 'I hope,' or 'I think,' but simply 'I KNOW that my Redeemer liveth.'

Dimly, as one groping his way through a fog, George began to realise the unspeakable consolation, the very balm of Gilead, which those words, coming down the ages through so many centuries, must bring to the heart of the mourner standing by the graveside of a loved one.

But a consolation that was not for him

Aileen was quick to perceive his distress, and was almost sorry that she had told him.

'Dear,' she said, 'you are not to grieve for me. It will upset me terribly if you think too much of what I have told you.'

'Do the others know?'

'No. I asked the doctor not to tell my husband yet. Later on, I will do so myself. I have confided in you because you knew my son, and for his sake I felt drawn to you. Now it is time you left me—I am tired.'

'Let me stay a while longer—I will be very quiet.'

'No—it is time you dressed for dinner. Go now, and you are not to worry.'

Reluctantly he left her, to go through what he considered the nonsensical rite of dressing for and eating a late dinner. He hated all that kind of thing on principle, but when it had been decided that he was to accompany his mother to Ballafagh, his uncle had told her to see to his wardrobe, giving her a cheque for all expenses. George did not know about the cheque, Anne having to say it was money of her own which she had by.

Except for this 'dressing up', as he contemptuously called it, and a few other items, George was not unhappy at Ballafagh. He had to admit that they were all kind to him, never by word or look, letting him see that they noticed his discrepancies in manner and speech.

Of course, it had been Rose who had persuaded him to come at all. She had laughingly talked him round, as perhaps no other could have done—not even his mother. The girl could turn him round her little finger, and knew it. Although she had refused him, let him plainly see that he was nothing to her, still he was not able to resist the fascination which she had for him.

'You must come and keep me company,' she had said, 'why, didn't you know I was going? Well, I am, and I will be a stranger there and so lonely if you don't come!'

Antoine had returned to Paris, and maybe George began to hope again in spite of common sense. Anyhow, he agreed to accompany his mother and the others to Ballafagh House. Although to all outward appearance, he and Rose were but friends, she still held him captive, and perhaps she did not object. She laughed at him with Nora, listening with mock solemnity to the lectures which the older woman considered it her duty to deliver, but yet she grew to like the young man during these days at Ballafagh more than she had done before.

They were thrown much together, exploring the grounds with eager delight. When George admired the gardens, and especially the Rosary, where the October roses still bloomed—veritable last roses of summer—Rose told him about the roses in France, and of the little house at Passy where she had been born, and where the roses climbed all over the wall.

'I was born in June, so Mamma called me Rose. Of course, there is a saint of that name, too, you know—St Rose of Lima.'

George made no reply. He never argued on religious matters with Rose. She had an uncanny way of ousting him by some unexpected remark, so that he had come to dread her sharp tongue when such questions were being discussed.

The first week of November came. Nora had returned to her work in Dublin, but Rose remained on at Ballafagh with Anne and George.

One afternoon Rose and George went for a walk along the road leading to Ballafagh. It was a damp day with signs of a coming fog. Rose, in a dark green coat with black furs, looked charming, and George, walking at her side, wished for the hundredth time that Antoine were at the bottom of the sea. As they turned to go home, the fog rose, as it were suddenly out of the ground, so that they could only see a few yards in front of them. To George, accustomed to the London 'peasoup' variety, it was no fog at all, but Rose did not like it and slipped her hand through his arm. The contact thrilled him, and made him feel nearer to her than ever before, and he thought to himself that at least they were real friends, if no more. And then some sudden impulse caused him to tell her, as a secret, about his aunt's health, and what she had said to him that evening as they sat by the fire.

She was at first dumbfounded; like him, she could hardly believe that it could be true, and when she realised that it might be so, she was overwhelmed with grief.

'Oh George, she is such a dear! I do hope it is not true! So lovely too, and young looking still. Before Hugh died, I have heard she was so young in appearance that she was like his sister. Can it be possible?'

'It is horrible,' replied George, 'I cannot bear to think of her lying in the grave—all the dreadful process of decay——'

'Oh, George, do not talk like that! How can you! Besides it will not be Aileen herself that will lie there. It will only be the husk of her real self. The soul will be with God.'

'Do you really believe in a life after death?'

'You know that I do. I am a Catholic.'

'I cannot believe in an existence after death. To me it will be the end of all things. Dust to dust again. "Imperial Caesar, dead and turned to clay, perchance may stop a hole to keep the wind away." Have I quoted correctly?'

'Oh, that old claptrap! Who minds that sort of thing? I wonder George, that you have not more sense than to be an atheist.'

'Sometimes I wish I could believe, but I cannot. That sort of spiritual dope is not for me.'

She turned upon him in sudden anger.

'The day will come when you will believe! I do not know how or why, but I feel that one day you will believe even as I do. You know I have these presentiments sometimes—and I have one now about you.'

He smiled and drew her more closely to his side.

'Rose,' he whispered, 'I am glad that you think of me at all. Sometimes it seems to me that you never think of me, while I— think of you every hour of every day.'

'How foggy it is,' she replied, wanting to change the conversation, 'I am always afraid of a fog.'

'Afraid of a fog? Why should you be? Besides this is nothing—you should see the fogs we have down Whitechapel way!'

'I always think that I will meet with an accident in a fog. Get run over or something. I often dream that this happens.'

'But Rose, you should not think such things! It is so foolish.'

'I am not half as foolish as you are anyway! And now I am going to promise you something, and that is, that if I die first—get run over or anything like that—I will come and tell you that there is a life after death. Then perhaps you will believe!'

'Rose—do not talk like that! I—I cannot bear to hear you——'

'Silly!' She glanced up at him with a smile that yet held a touch of sadness: 'Come on—let us hurry—it's time we were getting home. I want my tea!'

CHAPTER XVIII

THE PROMISE REDEEMED

Aileen Hewdon died in the following February. She faded away so imperceptibly that those who loved her could hardly believe that she was really gone. Her death took place in the early days of that month, which was cold and damp in Mayo, but the snowdrops were showing their white beauty in the gardens and grounds which she had loved so dearly, and they covered her coffin, so that it seemed that she had a pall of snow white.

Anne and Rose had been with her all the time. The sick woman took a great fancy to Rose; the girl was so bright and charming, her volatile gaiety and delightful mannerisms seemed to brighten up the old house, which had been quiet so long.

George had gone away in January—back to London. He told his mother that he was done with Ireland and the people, that they were superstitious fools upon whom he could make no impression. He would return to London, and take up work at their Headquarters there. All at Ballafagh House had tried to persuade him against this step, but in vain. Even Aileen could not prevail upon him to stay a while longer with her.

'It will not be for long,' she had said: 'I should like you to stay with me.'

'I am sorry—I must go.'

It was all he would say to all appeals.

Aileen, who understood him better than anyone else—not excepting his mother—knew that he was simply running away from influences which he feared: he was growing to love the house, the gardens, the ordered peace of it all. At the back of his mind the thought must have arisen: 'This may one day be my own.' To one imbued with his ideas and aims, this must have seemed like a temptation of the Evil One—had he believed in such a personage, which, of course, he did not. If he stayed longer, through the lovely spring time, into the glory of summer as it was in that lovely place, his will would surely weaken, he would become a traitor to the Cause which he had embraced so ardently. Only flight remained, and although he hated to leave Aileen in her present state of health, such a panic had come upon him, that he felt he must go away at all costs.

With Aileen the end came suddenly, as is often the way after a long illness. Victor had not time to send for George before she died, and his nephew would not come to the funeral. Victor was perfectly furious about this, and Anne terribly distressed. Only Rose, who had learned much of his character from Aileen, partly understood his motive for not coming.

'He could not bear it,' she said, 'you know, Major Hewdon, he has no belief in a life after the grave, and he loved her so much. Oh, it must be terrible for him!'

Rose was right. George had grown to love his uncle's wife very dearly, and he could not bear to follow her body to the grave. So he remained in London, having taken a room in Whitechapel, and there he flung himself into the propagandist work of the Communistic organisation.

He did not care for those with whom he worked; he never had done so, but now he realised that his heart was inclined to go over the sea to Ireland; now that he had seen with his own eyes the beauty of the Irish countryside, its imagery remained with him; like his poor father, who dying, had craved to see again the greens fields of Mayo, so too did his son, amidst the drab ugliness of Whitechapel, long to see the snow on the Mayo hills.

Here, in the great teeming city, he was alone, living in a ugly bed-sittingroom; hideous paper on the wall, rickety furniture, a gas ring to boil his kettle for breakfast. For his other meals he went to one of the cheap eating houses with which the district abounded, where he met other members of the organisation; men of various nationalities, although the larger number were Russian, many of them having been sent over to boost the happiness of people living under the Soviet Government.

At times he found himself wondering how it was that he did not take the same interest in his work as formerly, why these people were so distasteful to him? His own manners, even his accent, had sensibly improved so that some of his fellow-workers were now wont to utter disparaging remarks. It had transpired that he had been staying with his mother's people in Ireland—people of the so-called Capitalist class—and this did not make for friendship between George and the men with whom he worked.

He went to see his sister Mary, now married and settled in a small house with husband and baby. She was glad to see him, made him welcome in her shining kitchen, where she was preparing her husband's evening meal. However, when James Doran entered and saw George, he was decidedly cool to him, and afterwards told Mary that he would not have any of those 'blarsted Communists' in his house. So she had to give George a hint to this effect.

He was not in good health at this time, his food was poor; his lodgings comfortless. Often he would dream about Aileen; in some queer way she seemed to be near him. He put it all down to 'nerves', and got a tonic, but the dreams still continued.

In March, his mother wrote to say that Rose O'Daly had gone to Paris.

'She has not been looking well, Aileen's death upset her greatly. They were much attached to each other. However, Rose is getting to be her old self again now, and will be all right once she is back in her beloved Paris. Easter will soon be here, and she tells me that it is such a beautiful time over there. She has asked me to go over next year, and if all goes well, I should like to do so. And now about yourself——'

There followed the usual appeal that he would come 'home'— as his mother always called Ballafagh House. She told him that his uncle wished him to come and take his place as the heir to the property, and added her own request that he would do so. To all of which George made the usual reply that his work was in London, and there he would remain.

'I am glad you are happy in your old home,' he wrote, 'and you must be company for Uncle Victor. But Ballafagh House is no place for me—nor ever will be.'

So Rose had gone to Paris. He thought of her all that day, seeing her going shopping, walking on the Boulevards, or in the Champs Elysées, which she had so often described to him. She told him about the masses of flowers one could buy in Paris at Eastertide— above all the sweet scented narcissi of which she was so fond. Yes, he could see her there, in those surroundings which so suited her personality. Love and laughter seemed the very elements of which she was composed; one could never imagine her ill or sad; it was as if the fairies who came to her christening had said: 'We will never allow her to be gloomy or unhappy. All her life on earth shall be happy, and she shall bring happiness to others.'

As she had done—even to Aileen, during her last days on earth. It was Rose who had cheered her, brought a ray of sunlight into her life.

George hoped that Antoine would be good to her. He had the usual insular idea about Frenchmen, and hoped that this one would not break the heart of Rose O'Daly. If only she could have cared for him—George Dempsey—how willingly he would have put his two hands beneath her little feet.

Lent went by, and Easter was at hand. Holy Saturday was wet and dull. George felt depressed and miserable, and thought the reason must be that he had little to do. Everyone seemed busy with their own affairs, and he and his fellow Communists seemed out of place.

Early on Easter morning, George Dempsey awoke, thinking that some one had called him by name. He sat up in bed, peering around, as one will do when half asleep. Surely he had been called? And what was the perfume which seemed to fill the room. In a moment he recognised it for the scent of narcissi—strong, overpowering.

'George!'

The call had come again. It was early yet, but every object in the room was visible, and as his eyes took notice of the familiar surroundings, he saw something else. Someone was standing at the foot of his bed. It was Rose O'Daly. She was wearing a fur coat, and in her arms was a great sheaf of narcissi.

He stared at her, amazed, stupefied.

'Rose!' he whispered. Then: 'Is it really you?'

She stood there looking at him, her face serious and very pale—it seemed to George to be absolutely colourless.

'Rose—won't you speak to me?'

She spoke then, and although her voice seemed as if it came from a distance, the words were quite distinct.

'I have come to keep my promise. Pray for me.'

And while he was still looking at her, she was gone—faded into space, so that it was as if she had never been there.

'Rose! Where are you—come back to me—come back!'

Utter, complete silence. Could he have dreamt it? Was it an illusion? No—it was no illusion, for there still remained in the room the perfume of the flowers she had brought with her.

Realisation came but too quickly.

'Oh, Rose, my dear—my dear! You are gone too!'

Blindly he reached for his clothes, dressed and went into the dawn of the Easter morn. He walked on, not knowing or caring where his feet were leading him. People were abroad already, although it was barely six o'clock, and some instinct made him follow a little group who were entering a church. Mass was just commencing, and George Dempsey, the unbeliever, the Communist, knelt down and prayed for the soul of the woman whom he had loved on earth, and still loved in death.

As he was returning to his lodging, he came face to face with two of the Communist leaders—met them a few yards from the door of the church. They glanced significantly at each other, and then called out to George: 'Hello! Comrade. You are out early?'

'Yes—like yourselves,' replied George. He was still stupid, a trifle dazed, and did not in the least comprehend their attitude, or what it might mean.

'You were in that church?'

'Yes—I was at Mass,' he said, and passed on, leaving them to stare after him in amazed anger.

Two days later his mother wrote telling him that Rose O'Daly had been killed in a motor accident. She had been out in the afternoon of Holy Saturday, and was returning in the car with Antoine, her arms full of flowers which they had just bought, when there had been a collision with another car, and Rose was flung out and badly injured. She had been rushed to hospital, but died early on Easter Sunday.

'She was so fond of flowers, as you know,' added his mother; 'her coffin was one mass of narcissi and other spring blooms. Antoine wrote me all, he is heartbroken——'

George laid down the letter, he could read no more. What was Antoine's sorrow to his?

He applied for and was granted leave of absence from the organisation for which he worked. He said he was not in good health, and they believed him, for they could see it was true. He had always been a good worker for them, and really believed all that he advocated, which was more than could be said of many in the same organisation.

He left his lodgings and went to stay with his sister, while he was preparing to return to the Catholic Church. James Doran, inclined to be sceptical at first, gradually had his suspicions allayed, and realised that George was in earnest. Mary, delighted beyond words, poured forth her soul in thanksgiving. His mother, across the sea, was doing the same. They could hardly credit it; it was hardly to be believed. Only that they knew that with God all things are possible, they could not have had faith in his ultimate conversion.

But to George it was simply the logical conclusion, the sequel, to the message which he had received on Easter morning. He never doubted but that Rose had been with him, spoken to him, leaving behind her the scent of the narcissi which had been in her arms at the moment of the accident, and on her coffin afterwards. Dream, illusion, let it be what it might, to George Dempsey it was simple reality. A promise had been made to him one November evening on a road in Mayo, and it had been redeemed in a lodging-house in Whitechapel on Easter morn. Faith came to him as it comes to a little child.

To one of his character, there are no half measures. He was now as keen, as ardent a worker for the Catholic Church, as he had formerly been against her. He went to the Communist leaders for whom he worked, told them he was about to become a Catholic, and told them, too, that he meant to try and undo all the harm he had done in the past. They listened to him in silence; as it seemed to him, with indifference.

'I thought they would make no end of a fuss,' he said to Mary; 'there was a man last year—oh, well, that's another story. They didn't seem to mind about me, so I suppose I was not important enough to matter!'

James Doran, when alone with his wife, remarked that he did not like this attitude on the part of the Communist organisation.

'It would have been better if they had gone for him openly. To take it like that—well, I think it bodes no good for George.'

'But, Jim, you surely do not think——'

'I don't know what to think. But don't you worry. It may be O.K.'

George Dempsey made his Confession, and once more knelt at the altar to receive the Body and Blood of his Divine Master. This was early in May, and his mother crossed to London for the occasion. He was to return with her to Ballafagh House.

'Your uncle is so glad that you have given up your Communistic notions that he is even willing to forgive you for going back to the Church,' she said with a smile.

'I will be glad to see Ireland again,' said her son; 'isn't it strange, mother, how she pulls at one's heartstrings? I suppose it is my Irish

blood. I often think of poor father. I am sorry I treated him so badly.
I was sullen and unhappy all those years.'

'And I also,' replied Anne, 'I hated him at times. You see I was
only a Catholic in name for years. My faith meant little to me.'

'But I—I have been such an open enemy to the Church. How I
wish I could do something to undo the harm I have done!'

'Please God, so you will! Why—you have all your life before you.'

George was very happy on the day when he once again received
Holy Communion. It brought to his soul a sense of peace, of
happiness, such as he had never known before, but which is often
experienced by those who have been guided into the Fold of Peter,
almost against their own will. George was a generous giver, and
poured forth his love and devotion to the Divine Master. But, as
has been said, one cannot be generous with God; no matter how
much one gives, He will always give more in return. And so He
came, in tender love, with divine consolation, to George, as he
knelt in the little East End Church.

A happy day followed. There was quite a little festival in the
Doran's house, and George received many presents, including a
rosary, prayer book and other souvenirs of the day. He could not
but remember how short a while it was since he had sneered at all
such 'superstitious rubbish!'

'I am half sorry to be going home to Ireland,' he said that
evening, as they sat talking before going to bed, 'not that I am not
glad for my own sake—of course, I am. But there is so much to be
done here, and now that I understand and realise—oh, it seems as
if I should stay and give a helping hand. Especially as I have done
so much harm in the past.'

'Your duty is at Ballafagh,' said his mother, 'your uncle wants you
there, it is your heritage, where you will be master one day. You
must keep your word and return with me.'

'Oh yes—I mean to do so. Don't think I will not. It's only that I
know how much work can be done for Christ here.'

They were just about to retire for the night when a knock came
to the front door. James opened it, and came back with a note for
George.

'The messenger is waiting for a reply,' he said, and added, 'If I
were you, George, I would not bother about him. I know by the
looks of him that he's one of that lot!'

But when George read the note he stood up.

'I must go at once,' he said, 'this is to tell me that Sol Bernstein is ill—perhaps dying—and has asked for me. He and I were very friendly when I was in the Organisation.'

Doran followed him to the door, where a dark complexioned man of sullen aspect, was waiting for him.

'Look here,' whispered Doran, outside the kitchen door, 'I didn't want to frighten the women, but I don't like you going by yourself with this fellow. Let me come with you!'

George laughed heartily.

'Why, Jim! Do you think they are going to murder me? Do not worry—I will be home safe and sound. I cannot refuse poor Sol, we were such friends for years. Besides, I may be able to help him in some way.'

He was off before Jim could say any more, turning back to wave a cheery hand as he went.

His mother and Mary waited up for him until after one in the morning. Jim, who had to be up at six, went to bed. It was nearly two o'clock before Mary could persuade her mother to go to bed. And even then Anne did not sleep.

It was she who heard the knock which came about four in the morning. As she sprang from her bed to hasten downstairs, Mary came out of her room across the narrow landing, and went with her.

It was a policeman who stood there. He looked keenly at the two women, and then asked:

'Anyone of the name of Dempsey living here?'

'Yes,' answered Mary, 'my mother here is Mrs Dempsey.'

'Any others of the name?'

'My brother, George. He went out last night——'

She was interrupted by her mother.

'Is anything the matter? An accident? George is hurt—please tell me quickly!'

The man looked at her pityingly. These women were not the type that he had expected to meet. There was some mystery here.

'Well, missus, your son was shot last night. We have not found out who did it yet—but we will, you may be sure of that.'

'Shot? Is he badly wounded?' asked Mary.

But her mother gave a great cry.

'He is dead! My boy is dead!'

Mary looked piteously at the constable.

'Yes, he is dead,' he said, 'we found his body down Limehouse way, and there were letters in his pocket telling where he lived, and so on. I am sorry, missus——'

'If you will wait a moment—come in here, please—my husband will see you,' replied Mary, 'I must take mother to her room.'

When James Doran, hastily roused from sleep, came downstairs, the constable had little more to tell him. The body of George Dempsey had been discovered by the man on that beat. It was lying in an archway, and he had been shot through the heart, at such close range that his coat was scorched.

Doran told the constable about George's separation from the Communist organisation, and that supplied the motive at once.

'We will find whoever did it—you may be sure of that,' the man assured James Doran.

But the constable was wrong. The murderers of George Dempsey were never brought to justice, and after a short while his death was almost forgotten. It was the usual nine days' sensation, and then another murder, more terrible in detail, filled the front pages of the papers.

But Mary remembered him in her prayers, as she trod the London pavements to Mass in the church where he, too, had knelt at the altar but a few hours before he met his Saviour face to face.

And in Ireland, his mother never forgot him. If she sorrowed for him, she also rejoiced, so that her prayers and thanksgiving were mingled in one great act of worship to the God and Father of us all.

God had willed it so, and she would not have had it otherwise.

EPILOGUE

TEN YEARS AFTER

A boy on a pony was riding up the avenue to Ballafagh House—a boy about eight, dark haired, good-looking, sitting erect upon his mount with an easy grace that was all his own.

It was a morning in early June, and the great lilac bushes on each side of the avenue still shed their delicious perfume around; upon the windows of Ballafagh House, the sun was shining, giving promise of a warm day.

The boy took his pony round to the stables, and then entered the morning-room through the open window. His mother, seated at the breakfast table, turned to greet him with a smile.

'Had a nice ride, Desmond?'

'Yes, mother. I've been out since seven—it's a grand morning.'

'It is, indeed. You must have an appetite for breakfast—and here comes your father.'

Nora Hewdon was not greatly changed from the Nora Harding of ten years ago; rather plumper, more matronly, but as smilingly cheerful as ever, and with an expression of peace, of happiness, in the soft grey eyes which had not been there before.

Victor looked much older than his wife in spite of being several years younger. His face was lined and worn, he stooped slightly as he walked, and always serious and quiet, he now spoke little except to his wife. He had never really recovered from the death of Hugh. He knew he had not been to blame, yet the memory of it all was seared upon his mind, so that it could never be forgotten or erased. Ten years ago. Still at times he would dream of the road outside Margallin, and the brave young heart who had been killed in the ambush there—killed when he—the boy's father—had given the order to fire. Even his wife found it difficult at times to turn his thoughts away from the remembrance of that terrible period.

Except for that haunting memory, Victor was as happy as any man could hope to be. He and Nora were married nine years ago and had one child, the boy whom we have met. He was called

'Desmond', because it had been the second name of that other lad whom both had loved so dearly.

Victor had married Nora, agreeing to the conditions against which he had rebelled so long ago. Desmond was brought up in the Catholic Faith, taught Irish ideals, spoke the old Gaelic tongue fluently. His father never made any objection; he had given his word to Nora before their marriage that if God blessed them with children, she should have the training of them, and that they should be Catholics. If, at times, he wondered what his ancestors would say could they know that the heir to Ballafagh, the next Master of Hewdon, was a Catholic and a 'rebel', he kept all such thoughts to himself. Not even to her whom he loved above all else on earth, did he breathe a word. Not that she did not know. She could read him like a book, but being a wise woman never spoke of such things. She only stormed Heaven more fervently for the soul of the man who was dearer to her than life itself.

'Is Aunt Anne not down yet?' asked Desmond.

Even as he spoke the door opened, and Anne Dempsey entered. An elderly woman now, and looking older than her age. Otherwise she seemed more content, happier than she had been for years. The sorrow she had felt for the loss of her son had been softened, turned to thanksgiving for the wonderful grace which he had received. She sometimes spoke of it to Nora, marvelling at the Mercy of God, who had given this grace to one who for so long had been an enemy of Christianity.

'Saul, Saul, why persecutest thou Me?'

Wonderful forgiveness, that the soul of such a man should be summoned to meet his Saviour a few hours after his reconciliation to the Church.

Anne love Desmond, and the child returned her affection. She would have spoiled him had Nora allowed her, but she was too wise a mother for that, and to Desmond, while he loved his aunt, there was no one in all the world just like 'mammy'. He was beginning to call her 'mother' now, he was getting such a big boy, a child no longer in his own estimation. His affection for his father was tinged with a certain amount of fear; not that Victor was ever harsh or severe, but he simply did not understand children; to him the heart of a child would always be a sealed page.

This morning Desmond's mind was so occupied with one thing that he said to his father at once:

'Are you coming to the Feis, Daddy?'

Victor Hewdon looked at his son for a moment without speaking. There was a Feis in the Convent grounds that afternoon, and he knew that Desmond was to dance and recite. Even now, he could not grow used to the thought; it seemed incredible that his son should be there, dancing, playing games, mixing with the people.

'I don't think so, Desmond.'

'Oh—Daddy!'

Acute disappointment was in the boy's voice. He had so wanted his father to see him dancing—why, he hoped to win a medal!

Nora glanced across the table at her husband.

'Perhaps you will be able to come after all,' she said, 'I know you are busy today, but Desmond wants you to see how well he can dance.'

Anne said nothing. She took no interest in politics—to her the world was gone mad—and all that mattered to her now was her love for her family, and the consolations of her religion.

But Victor found himself that afternoon standing beside his wife in the Convent grounds, watching his son dance and play and recite in the Gaelic. All around him he heard the soft Gaelic tones, saw the children in the Gaelic costumes.

'How well Desmond looks in the kilts!' remarked Nora, her eyes following her son as he took his place amongst the dancers.

'He always looks well,' replied Victor, 'he is a fine boy.'

Nora smiled at him shyly, reminding him of the Nora whom he had wooed long ago in the Nurse's Cottage at Larramore.

'I am glad you are pleased with him,' she said, 'and although I know that there are certain things about which you and I differ, still——'

'One must move with the times, you would say? I suppose it is true. A new Ireland has come to life—or, as I know you would say— the old one is alive again. Well, I suppose one must conform to all that. But it is not easy for me.'

Nora slipped her hand within his arm.

'Your son died to help to make the new Ireland,' she said, 'do not forget that, Victor.'

'I do not forget. But as for Desmond—I hope he will live for it!'

'I think he will,' replied Nora, 'just look at him!'

The Feis was over, and the band were playing the 'Soldier's Song.' They watched Desmond as he stood at attention, erect, rigid, his straight little body and fine legs showing to advantage in the national dress.

Above them waved the Tricolour, and Victor Hewdon, remembering a boy who had died in order that that Flag might wave over his country, bared his head, and he, too, stood at attention until the last notes of the National Anthem had died on the breeze.

The Walk of a Queen

Annie M. P. Smithson

In *The Walk of a Queen* the scene is set in Dublin during the War of Independence and it is a fascinating story of passion and intrigue which holds the reader's interest from start to finish.

The Weldons of Tibradden

Annie M. P. Smithson

The Weldons of Tibradden follows the fortunes of three generations of the Weldon family beginning in the 1870s and ending in 1935. It is a fascinating story of success, courage, love and betrayal.

Her Irish Heritage

Annie M. P. Smithson

Her Irish Heritage, a story of love and courage, is now reprinted for the benefit of new generations who did not have an opportunity to read it.

Great Irish Love Stories

Una Morrissy

A dashing and wealthy young nobleman and a hauntingly beautiful girl of mysterious origins meeting in Paris at the height of the French Revolution suggests the first instalment of a lush romantic serial. But it really happened! The love story of Lord Edward and Pamela, set here in the context of that dramatic period, was as true and loyal as the political background against which they moved was treacherous.

The woman in John Mitchel's life was made of sterner stuff. "Pretty Jenny Verner" was only sixteen when she fell in love with that incorruptible and fiery champion of causes, cast in a hero's mould. For thirty-eight years of their married life she supported him through prison, transportation, escape and exile, involvement in the American Civil War, family tragedy and even shipwreck. The stirring story of John and Jenny is quite a parable for modern times.

Here too are the enigmas of James Clarence Mangan and his lost love, and of Jonathan Swift and Stella.

Perhaps the liveliest of all is the warm and sunny story of the elopement and marriage of the irrepressible Richard Brinsley Sheridan and his truly lovely bride, Elizabeth Linley, the nightingale of Bath.

The Red-Haired Woman and other Stories

Sigerson Clifford

"He blamed Ellie for his failure to sell. She stood before him on the road that morning, shook her splendid mane of foxy hair at him and laughed. He should have returned home straightaway and waited 'till she left the road. It was what the fishermen always did when they met her. It meant bad luck to meet a red-haired woman when you went fishing or selling. Everyone knew that . . ."

"This collection of stories has humour, shrewd observation, sharp wit at times, and the calm, sure touch of the accomplished storyteller . . . You will remember *The Red-Haired Woman, Master Melody, The Spanish Waistcoat, The Rebel* and *Randal's Ring* long after you've forgotten the big blaring headlines that assault your eyes contemplating the morning paper" (from the 'Introduction' by Brendan Kennelly)